REAPERS & READING

A LIBRARY WITCH MYSTERY
BOOK SIXTEEN

ELLE ADAMS

Hosting a party in a magical library came with certain hazards.

When the first guests came through the front doors, they were greeted with a loud hooting sound, courtesy of the topmost decoration on one of the twin Christmas trees that dominated the lobby. In place of an angel sat a giant tawny owl: Sylvester, the resident spirit of the library itself. Otherwise known as a genius loci, he spent his time masquerading as a talking owl for reasons known only to himself, and he wanted to ensure everyone paid more attention to him than they did to the regular festivities. The noise certainly got their attention. A few people jumped, startled, then laughed when the hooting turned into a jolly chant of "Ho, ho, ho!"

Fake snow began to fall from the ceiling, a veritable blizzard of sparkling flakes that blanketed everything in seconds. Luckily, the guests took the stunt in good humour and were soon laughing and singing along to the Christmas music that sprang up from the speakers my Aunt Adelaide had installed on the balconies up on the second floor.

Every year, the library's decorations were a sight to behold. Aside from the giant glittering trees, tinsel draped the tall bookshelves, and mistletoe festooned the balconies on the three floors above. There was technically a fourth floor, too, but that wasn't visible from this angle, and fortunately, none of our visitors had found their way up there since the mishap a few weeks before. It had been Estelle's idea to host a solstice party so that we could take our minds thoroughly off those events, with the bonus of drawing attention to the library for a positive reason rather than a negative one.

We'd succeeded in both aspects. Aunt Candace had mostly stopped sulking in her room, though she'd stopped short of making a proper showing at the event and was instead partaking in her usual habit of lurking behind bookshelves, fishing for gossip.

Her older sister, my Aunt Adelaide, swept around, cleaning up spilled drinks, refreshing the buffet table, and moving any obstacle that the library threw into the way when one of the guests unwittingly stepped out of bounds. Her eldest daughter, my cousin Estelle, presided over the celebrations, accompanied by Spark, her pixie assistant. She wore a dress that glittered with red and silver to match her mother's, and since they shared the same curly red hair and curvy figures, they might have been twins.

My cousin Cass was absent, but that wasn't conspicuous by any means. She spent most of her time ensconced up on the third floor with her animals and was even less of a party animal—pun intended—than her pet manticore.

I wasn't into parties that much myself, but my best friend, Laney, had always been able to drag me out of whichever corner I was hiding in to join in the fun. She showed up shortly after the dancing kicked off, dressed in a shimmering black-and-silver number made all the more striking given her vampire's grace and balance. As she was most active at sundown, she was in her element, her eyes bright and her mouth stretched in a grin that exposed her pointed fangs.

Before I'd quite realised what she was doing, Laney took my hand and dragged me into a dance. Vampires' movement made me feel like a clumsy ogre in comparison, but the darkness made any self-consciousness unnecessary. It was fun twirling around with her and laughing, forgetting all our troubles—at least until I spied a pair of eyes watching me from between the branches of the tree.

I glanced up, confirming Sylvester was still on top of the tree, not inside.

Laney noticed my line of sight and peered closer. "It's your cousin."

So it was. The eyes blinked then vanished, but I'd already glimpsed a piece of Cass's red hair through the gap in the branches. "Cass, what are you doing inside Sylvester's tree?"

"Nothing!" she said in snappish tones. "He stole my glasses."

"I most certainly did not." The owl's indignant reply drifted down from above. "She's lying."

Cass made an irritated noise. "What does it matter? Go on, get back to partying."

"What are you up to in there?" She hadn't brought the manticore downstairs, had she?

No response came, and when Laney pulled the branches apart, I was unsurprised to see that Cass had vanished entirely.

"Weird." I stepped back as the branches snapped back into place. "What's up with her?"

"Maybe she wanted to join in the dancing but was too shy."

"Pretty sure Cass has never been shy in her life." More likely, she'd been curious about the party but not enough to break her habit of lurking in the background, judging everyone rather than joining in the fun. "I was worried she'd lost an animal in there, but I guess not."

"Would the manticore even fit?" Laney asked dubiously.

"Probably best not to think too hard about that." Sylvester would certainly object to a manticore—or any other magical monster, for that matter—sitting in his tree, but even Cass wouldn't go as far as to smuggle in a new friend during a party with hundreds of guests present. I hoped.

"Hmm." Laney watched the tree with a thoughtful expression on her face then shrugged. "Back to dancing?"

"Sure." Just then, I spied someone else standing near the library's front door, his silhouette noticeable even in the darkness outside the spotlights on the dance floor.

It was kind of embarrassing that after nearly a year of officially being together, my breath still caught whenever I set eyes on Xavier unexpectedly. He was as striking as a vampire, at least in my opinion, with blond curls tumbling over eyes a startling shade of aquamarine. His face broke into a smile when he spotted me, and my heart skipped a beat.

"Oh, you'll want to dance with him instead." Laney slipped me a wink and sashayed away, catching the arm of a passing witch and drawing her into a kind of half waltz, half foxtrot. Any kind of dance looked effortlessly elegant with a vampire at the wheel.

I ducked my head as I walked over to the door, conscious that a fair few people had turned to watch me approach Xavier. It wasn't just his strikingness that drew attention but the scythe he carried strapped to his back, along with the fact that he could have just as easily stepped out of thin air as through the front door.

"Hey," I said. "Glad you could make it."

"Rory." He took my hand and kissed me on the lips. "I can only stay an hour. I hope that's all right."

"Of course." It was lucky he'd shown up at all, given how controlling his Reaper boss could be, and it was probably better that he wasn't around when Aunt Candace inevitably got into the punch bowl and started asking all our visitors intrusive questions. "Something came up with your boss?"

"Kind of." He brushed a few fake snowflakes off my shoulder. "I should probably explain somewhere less public."

That figures. This time last year, Grim Reaper had gone as far as to force his apprentice to leave town altogether, with the implication that they would never return, and while he'd shown no signs of repeating that performance, it would explain why I felt a flutter of apprehension as I followed Xavier into the living room. My family's living quarters lay down a corridor off the lobby and consisted of a small, cosy living room and kitchen with stairs leading up to our bedrooms. Though the walls weren't soundproofed, the noise from the party was notably muted once we sat down on the sofa. Honestly, I was starting to get a little nervous at how he was going about this, as if he was about to drop some dreadful revelation on my head. We'd been through so much together already, I knew, but my nerves thrummed as I sat down to wait for him to speak.

"I already told you it's tradition for all the local Reapers and their apprentices to meet for a summit at the end of each year, didn't I?"

"Possibly?" Last year, he hadn't actually *been* here, and he usually had to give away the bare minimum of details in order to avoid ticking off his cranky boss, the aptly named Grim Reaper. "Does that mean you're going away?"

"No," he said. "It means the other local Reapers and their apprentices are coming here to Ivory Beach."

"There are other Reapers coming *here*?"

"Four of them," he said. "Plus their apprentices. The boss

isn't happy that our home was volunteered, but we typically take it in turns, and Ivory Beach came up next on the list."

"I didn't know our town was a contender."

Four Reapers? Aside from Xavier and his boss, the only other one I'd met had been working for the enemy. And Maura, a half-Reaper who'd given up her apprenticeship to become a freelance ghost hunter, didn't really count either.

"That's right," he said. "They'll be here until the New Year, so I figured I'd warn you in advance."

"I'm amazed you were allowed to come to the party, then," I remarked. "I would have thought your boss would make you stay at home to prepare."

"He tried," said Xavier. "The thing is, there's not much to actually *do*. Reapers don't require a welcoming committee."

I snorted. "No, I guess not. I suppose you don't have to worry about having enough bedrooms or food supplies in the house, given that Reapers don't need either."

"Exactly," he confirmed. "Though I'll still be expected to keep the apprentices entertained while our bosses are engaged in top-secret meetings."

"You aren't invited?" I blinked in surprise. "I would have thought your boss would want you to know anything that might be important and relevant to both of you."

"He usually does," he said. "This is secretive Council business, though, and some of the other Reapers have more traditional ideas about what they're allowed to share with their apprentices. They also tend to disagree a lot, so we decided it would be easier just to play along."

I raised an eyebrow. "Wait, there's someone out there who's even *more* secretive and grumpy than your boss is?"

"You'd be surprised," he said lightly. "We're Reapers. Secretive and grumpy kind of goes with the territory."

"I hope the apprentices aren't the same."

"I don't think they are," he said. "Actually, I wondered if

you might like to meet them. Since we'll be shut out of half the meetings, I figured they might want to go on a tour of Ivory Beach and see the sights."

"You want me to give a bunch of Reaper apprentices a tour of the town?" I couldn't quite keep the scepticism from my voice. There wasn't a great deal to do in Ivory Beach at this time of year anyway, and it seemed unlikely that they'd want me to take them to eat ice cream on the pier or to go for drinks at the local pub.

"If you want," he said. "They're going to be here for a few days, and it would be good to have company."

"I guess most Reaper apprentices don't get out much." I'd grown so accustomed to Xavier being the only apprentice Reaper I knew that I'd forgotten there'd be others in his position, though Xavier was unique as far as Reaper apprentices went, having been abandoned by his human family and essentially adopted by the Grim Reaper as a consequence. It seemed a hell of a lonely childhood to me, and it still amazed me that Xavier had grown up as a relatively normal person— if you discounted the scythe and the ability to walk through walls, that is.

"I think they'd be excited to meet you," he said. "Anyway, it's up to you. I thought you might like to show them the library."

"I'd have to ask my aunt." The library was the town's main attraction, the store of all the knowledge in the magical world that my family had managed to catalogue—yet for all that, there weren't any books about Reapers hidden within its walls. While the vampires had mostly failed in their attempts to prevent the library from getting hold of their secrets, the Reapers were a different story, and any books that existed were in their hands alone.

As for our own books, after our recent narrow escape, my family members were given to caution, but they wouldn't want visitors to the town to feel unwelcome either. I was sure my aunt would be happy to let our guests see the sights.

I rose from the sofa and spied Laney lurking outside the living room. When I beckoned, she walked in, offering a fanged smile to Xavier. "What are you doing in here? Aren't you coming back to the party?"

"Xavier's boss has guests coming to town," I explained. "There's a Reaper summit at his house. He invited me to meet the other apprentices and show them around Ivory Beach tomorrow."

"Ooh." Aunt Candace popped up in the doorway as if she'd been lurking there the whole time. "Do tell."

"What's going on?" The noise—or Aunt Candace's general aura of trouble—had drawn Aunt Adelaide too.

It would be easier to explain to everyone together, so I gave them a brief overview of what Xavier had told me.

"They want to see the library?" Concern flickered across Aunt Adelaide's face. "That ought to be fine as long as we take some precautions."

"And avoid the upper floors," I guessed. "We can do that."

"They might not be interested in reading any of the books," Xavier said. "It's okay if you don't want them in here. There's plenty to see in the rest of Ivory Beach. I just didn't want to involve Rory without telling you first."

"Obviously, she wants to," said Aunt Candace. "She's going to bring back a full report too. In fact, I'll send my notebook and pen along to make sure she doesn't miss anything."

"That's enough," said Aunt Adelaide. "We'll talk about this later. Candace, stop badgering Rory and get back to the party."

"We should do the same," Xavier murmured to me. "Also, you really don't have to volunteer as tour guide. I know you want to spend time with your family during the holidays."

"I want to meet the others." I could hardly go the entire holiday season without seeing Xavier at all, and my curiosity about the other Reapers was undiminished.

"Of course," said Aunt Adelaide. "If they want a tour of the library, I don't see why not. Maybe avoid going higher than the second floor, though."

"Good call." Cass might not react well to Reapers treading near her haven in the Magical Creatures Division, which was also entirely too close to the entrance to the fourth-floor corridor for comfort. A corridor that could grant wishes might be of little interest to most Reapers, but its mysterious guardian would certainly object to the intrusion regardless. Besides, there were plenty of curiosities on the other floors. "I'd better tell Estelle too."

It was somewhat difficult to speak to my cousin while enveloped in the full noise of the party, but I managed to signal to her to come to the other side of the room.

"What is it?" She reached my side and raised her voice over the general clamour. "Something came up with Xavier?"

I explained, having to backtrack a couple of times due to the music drowning out my voice. "Aunt Adelaide said it's okay if we bring them into the library to show them around, but I wanted to check with you too."

"Of course," she said. "Nobody who comes to Ivory Beach isn't curious about the library."

"I thought… you know, that the fourth floor's guardian might object."

"It's never objected to Xavier coming in here," she reminded me. "We can block that area off. It'll be fine. If they get to have their secrets, so do we."

True. And who knew, it might be the Grim Reaper who put his foot down. He was touchy about humans getting involved in Reaper business at the best of times, and my relationship with Xavier had put me in his crosshairs, but my family had been entangled with the Reapers before I'd even been aware the magical world existed. My dad had run into the Reapers a few times in the years he'd spent accidentally ticking off a certain group of rogue vampires in his quest to acquire rare books. That I'd stumbled into the middle of the same conflict myself was not a point in my favour, but after a great deal of turmoil, the Grim Reaper had grudgingly come to accept that Xavier and I were together for the long haul—provided, that was, I didn't ask too many questions.

As for the other Reaper apprentices, they might be able to give me some valuable inside information that their supervisors refused to divulge, such as the nature of the history between my dad and the Grim Reaper himself, topics I generally avoided in a bid to keep the peace.

"Hey." Xavier took my hand. "Ready to dance?"

I shoved the stack of questions back into the recesses of my mind and fixed a smile on my face. "Sure."

2

Heavy rain woke me up at dawn after an already restless night, in part due to the amount of tinsel that had somehow ended up in my bed and in part because of my upcoming meeting with the Reapers from out of town. My dreams had been haunted by shadowy figures wielding scythes, and I found myself glad that we'd mutually agreed to close the library the following day to clean up the aftermath of the party.

I sat down to a late breakfast with an equally sleepy Estelle and poured myself a liberal amount of coffee.

"Trouble sleeping?" she asked sympathetically. "Me too. I think the guests upset the books. A volume of alchemy showed up in my room and kept wailing at me until I took it back to the correct shelf. On the third floor."

I scratched the back of my shoulder. "I guess I should be glad I only had tinsel in my bed. Though it itches like hell."

"Tell me about it." She stifled a yawn and bit into a piece of toast. "My mum was up the latest, I think. She had to throw out some drunk werewolves who showed up just as the party was ending and tried to stage a climbing contest on Sylvester's tree."

"They're lucky he didn't dive-bomb them." I applied jam to my own toast, glad that with magic at our disposal, cleaning up the library would take a matter of hours instead of days and was infinitely less inconvenient, screaming books aside.

"You can still go to Xavier's," added Estelle. "We have the full day off, so there's plenty of time for us to set the place in order."

"Yes." Aunt Adelaide entered the kitchen and helped herself to a plate. "We prepared well, so it's just the lower floor that needs a little tidying up. You can go to Xavier's whenever you need to."

"I'm not sure what time the Reapers will actually show up." Xavier had gone home from the party early, which suggested they'd arrive either at night or very early in the morning. Nighttime was more in character for the Reapers, though not as much as for the vampires. "It's probably for the best that they didn't arrive in the middle of the party."

"A wasted opportunity if you ask me." Aunt Candace entered, wearing one of her bright flowery dressing gowns. "Oh, someone already made coffee. Excellent."

"You're welcome." Estelle yawned again and rose to her feet. "I'm going to check there aren't any more screaming books in the lobby."

"There aren't. I looked." Aunt Adelaide piled toast on her plate and sat down on my other side. "There *is* a substantial amount of tinsel on the stairs, but it didn't make it up to the third floor."

"Cass probably put a shielding spell outside the Magical Creatures Division." After her odd behaviour the previous day, she never had come back to the party, so I'd assumed she'd gone straight back to her favourite haunt. "The animals weren't disturbed?"

"Aside from Sylvester. He threw so much tinsel at the werewolves that they left a trail all the way across the square."

"The rain'll wash it away," Aunt Candace said cheerfully, pouring coffee into a mug three times the size of mine. "I like this weather. It's very atmospheric for what I'm writing."

"Glad someone's enjoying it." Taking the Reaper apprentices on tour in the pouring rain wasn't appealing, but neither was spending hours in the Grim Reaper's central-heating-free house either.

"Since you're in such a good mood, you're going to help me tidy up the library, aren't you?" Aunt Adelaide asked her sister.

"Only when I've finished my book," she proclaimed. "It's a tragic tale of angst and deceit, and I need to finish writing it while I'm in the mood."

"As long as she sticks to writing and not expressing herself in other ways," I muttered as she left the kitchen with the coffee pot in one hand and her giant mug in the other. "I know it's better if she pours her angst into a book instead of raining it all over the library."

Literally, my aunt's infamous temper tantrums tended to involve unplanned indoor weather events. They'd been especially frequent since she'd conjured one of her book characters to life a few weeks before and he'd subsequently betrayed her trust, though the previous night's party seemed to have improved her mood notably.

Admittedly, it was outdoor weather events that concerned me more than indoor ones, given the current storm outside. Rain lashed against the windows, and the wind battering the walls crept through every gap and crevice.

I'd layered on every piece of knitwear I owned beneath the long cloak that formed the main part of my uniform, and the chill somehow crept in. I was nursing my third hot chocolate when I heard the knock on the front door shortly before noon.

I opened the door to a slightly damp Xavier, but before I could greet him, Aunt Candace appeared at my back with her notebook and pen bouncing at her side. "He's here. Excellent."

"I told you that you can't come with us, Aunt Candace," I said out of the corner of my mouth. "Anyway, I thought you were finishing a book."

"I couldn't miss the grand tour, could I?"

"Actually, there's been a change of plans, given the weather is less than ideal for sightseeing," Xavier said mildly. "And my boss has been pretty clear that I'm not to bring anyone except Rory into the house."

"That's right," Aunt Adelaide came over, casting a warning look at her sister. "Good to see you, Xavier. No trouble, is there?"

"No, except that we're postponing the tour until the weather's calmed down a bit," he said. "Some of the apprentices don't mind, given that we can't feel the cold, but it'd be unfair to Rory."

"What's the alternative plan?" I asked. "I'm going to come to your house and hang out with the apprentices?"

"If you don't mind," he said. "They're excited to meet you."

"All right." I had a hard time believing that, but it would be nice to have a few allies among the Reapers' ranks, if just to counter the inevitable attitude problems I'd encounter from the Grim Reaper's counterparts. If they shared his feelings concerning my involvement in matters that were supposed to be confined to the Reapers alone, I was in for a rough time.

I grabbed an umbrella first and cast a windproof spell on it to counter the gale that tried to sweep us off our feet as we left. Holding the umbrella like a shield, Xavier and I walked across the town square toward the adjacent high street on which the cemetery was located.

"Fair warning—my boss might want to speak to you first," said Xavier. "The others have been asking questions that I didn't want either of us to answer without your input."

"Oh no." I lifted my umbrella to dislodge a stray piece of tinsel that was no doubt a souvenir from the party the previous night. "I thought your boss was only going to tell them the bare minimum about… you know. Us."

"It's been hard for him to avoid certain topics," he said, "such as the Founders and the fact that the pair of us are known to be on their list of targets."

A shiver trailed down my spine. "That, and… I guess he had to tell the others about that potion even if there isn't any of it left."

"It was also hard to justify not mentioning the rogue Reaper too," he said. "The good news is that the rogue was apprehended shortly after Carlos Verdant's arrest, according to the others. She's no longer a threat."

"That's good to hear." I'd almost forgotten all about the rogue Reaper since Xavier and Maura had thoroughly sent her packing more than two months before. I'd figured that she was lying low after the Founders' arrest, and having one fewer enemy to worry about was more than welcome. "Did your boss tell everyone the Founders were brewing potions designed to work on Reapers yet, though?"

"He did, and that's what led to their disagreement," said Xavier. "Shaw's supplies were destroyed, and we have no proof that he ever made them widely available. That's why you'll probably be asked to give testimony. I've already had to answer a bunch of questions myself."

Oh boy. We ducked through the gate into the cemetery and walked past rows of silent graves toward the large, grand house at the back. Despite its impressive stature, the house had a distinct air of neglect and rivalled the vampires' place for creepiness. The interior was colder than the rest of town no matter the season, while the rooms were austere and without any human adornment or personality.

The same could be said for the tall, shadowy figure with a large scythe strapped to his back who greeted us at the door. Since he kept his face hidden most of the time, it was hard to tell what the Grim Reaper was thinking except when he was *really* mad. Then everyone knew to run to the hills.

"Aurora," he said in cold, resonant tones. "The others have requested to meet you. They're in the main room."

Hello to you, too. I bit back the response, reasoning that the Grim Reaper was bound to be in a tetchy mood with a bunch of curious strangers in the house, asking nosy questions. I had zero desire to become an outlet for his annoyance, whether it took the form of barbed words or an even sharper stick.

The Grim Reaper glided ahead of Xavier and me through a door off the hallway into a room whose only furnishings were a long wooden table lined with uncomfortable hard-backed chairs.

And in each chair sat a Reaper.

At first glance, they might have appeared human despite the fact that all except one of them wore the stereotypical black hooded cloak that characterised the Reaper I knew well. If they'd had their hoods up like him, it would have been impossible to tell them apart save for their height. One was shorter and stockier than the others, an appropriately grim-faced old man with a deep scowl etched on his milk-pale face. On his right-hand side sat a surprisingly young woman with a streak of pink in her dyed-black hair and an array of silver rings on her thin, pale fingers. She flashed me a smile that had an almost mischievous edge.

On the table's other side, a stately-looking woman dressed like she was attending a high-class funeral was seated next to a slightly younger man who had what appeared to be a giant wolfhound lying next to his chair. When the beast saw me, it rose onto four vast paws and growled, exposing vampire-sharp teeth. I hovered in the doorway, wondering why in the world I'd agreed to this.

"You must be Aurora." The younger-looking woman spoke first, tilting her head on one side. "You're the human who fought the Founders."

The Grim Reaper swept past and positioned himself at the head of the table. Xavier didn't join him, instead picking out two of the remaining seats nearest the door for the pair of us. Sitting was no more comfortable than standing since the wooden chairs were the sort you'd find in a picture of a Victorian household rather than an actual home, and the Reapers' stares only intensified now that I was on the same level as them.

I stifled a shiver, clearing my throat. "Hello. I'm Aurora Hawthorn, but I usually go by Rory."

"You're from the library," said the grim-faced old man. "I've heard a lot about that place."

"As have I," said the younger woman, whose smile looked almost genuine. "I'm Valkyrie, but you can call me Val. It's a pleasure to finally meet you."

"You too," I said, surprised at her friendly tone. The others, by contrast, eyed me with distrust or plain indifference.

"I am Gwyn," said the man with the giant wolfhound. "This is Hunt."

Hoping that name wasn't a portent of what might be to come, I shifted my seat a little to ensure my feet were out of reach of those razor-sharp teeth.

"I am Freya," said the older woman, leaning forward slightly and exposing the large scythe strapped to her back. "You're not what I expected. Did you really fight a vampire?"

"Yes." I decided not to add *Several, in fact.* "With help."

"No doubt," said the older man, who had yet to introduce himself. "You work at the library, as I understand it?"

"That old grump is Janus," put in Val. "And yes, we already established the library is Rory's home. She's not here to move in on our territory."

"What?" I looked at Xavier, alarmed. "Of course I'm not."

"We also weren't aware this was an interrogation," Xavier put in. "It's not appropriate for all five of you to harass a human who hasn't committed a crime."

"On the contrary," said Janus, "we have all heard stories out of this town that are worthy of a visit from the Reaper Council, and this young woman and her family seem to be at the centre."

A visit from the Reaper Council? My palms went sweaty. Attention from the higher-ups amid the Reapers' ranks was precisely what Xavier and I had been trying to avoid.

"The Reaper Council has no reason to visit this town," said the Grim Reaper. "The Founders' local bases have been purged and their inhabitants arrested. It is their allies with whom the Council must concern themselves. I brought this human here to corroborate my apprentice's account of a concerning incident a few weeks ago."

"It sounds like the human and your apprentice both became entangled in this incident without your knowledge," said Freya. "Do you often allow your apprentice to operate independently?"

My hands fisted at my sides. I'd known, on some level,

that the Grim Reaper extended more freedom to his apprentice than some of his companions, but I couldn't help feeling a little sorry for whoever had the misfortune to be tied to her for the next few hundred years or more.

"My apprentice was investigating the vampires on my orders," said the Grim Reaper testily. That wasn't true, but I certainly wasn't going to contradict him. "I do not need to watch his every move in order to believe his word."

"He claims there were certain *potions* being developed by the Founders, potions designed to be used on Reapers." Scepticism dripped from Gwyn's voice. "You cannot provide us with a sample?"

"They were destroyed." I spoke up since it seemed like they were never going to get round to the *questioning Rory* part without prompting on my end. "I can back up Xavier's story, though. They also have poisons designed to put even vampires into an eternal sleep, and the one they tested on Xavier looked like the same sort but for Reapers instead."

I'd expected that part to get a reaction, and sure enough, the others all began talking at once. Xavier and I were all but forgotten as they flung accusations back and forth for a good fifteen minutes before Val glanced my way and snapped her fingers.

"I'll escort the human out, shall I?" she said, rising from her seat. "I'm sure she has more exciting plans for her afternoon than witnessing you lot raging at one another."

I hesitated when Val took my arm and tried to pull me to my feet, but the Grim Reaper hadn't wanted me there in the first place, and it was plain that the others thought of me as some kind of mixture between an interloper and a dangerous interference—so, just like the Grim Reaper had seen me at first, in other words. When Xavier got to his feet, too, I followed him and Val from the room.

"Sorry about them," she said. "I told them not to be so

harsh, but they never listen to me. Especially Janus. He's always suspicious of anyone who manages to survive a trip into the afterworld, considering so many of his own apprentices have a nasty habit of dying in there."

"They… what?"

"Don't worry. It isn't catching." She winked. "As for Charon, I'd never believe he'd let *his* apprentice pursue a relationship with a human if I hadn't seen it for myself."

"Who's Charon?" Hang on a moment. "The Grim Reaper? That's his name?"

"He never told you?" She snickered. "Isn't that just like him?"

"Guess they can't all be called the Grim Reaper," I said. "Is that his actual name or just a nickname? The name is from Greek mythology, right?"

"We often choose a new name when we take up Reaper training," she explained. "Or a title if we're feeling particularly egotistical. It's easier to sever ties with our human lives that way."

"Ah." My gaze flickered toward Xavier, who'd moved further down the dimly lit hallway. "He didn't. Did he?"

"Oh, apprentices sometimes keep their human names for a while. Like a trinket from their old lives. They get over it." A wistful expression came over her. "Not like they have much choice. I wanted to call myself Terror of the Night when I took my master's place, but the Council wouldn't let me."

"When you took your master's place?" I asked. "When does that happen? And… what does your master do, retire?" Was retirement an option for a Reaper? They were essentially immortal, after all.

"If you live for long enough, you eventually grow tired of it. Or so I'm told. Most Reapers back out by choice, or else they… I probably shouldn't be talking about this with a human."

"I guess not," I said awkwardly.

"Anyway, you should go and meet the others. They're more like you. Human… well, not exactly, but more human than that lot." She jerked her thumb toward the meeting room.

Right. I spied Xavier waiting near the living room door and excused myself to join him. When he pushed the door open, I spied three strangers seated in the various armchairs, all as disarmingly ordinary in appearance as their masters.

One was a pale, twitchy-looking young man in his late teens or early twenties, dressed in some kind of high-collared outfit that made him look more like an apprentice vicar than an apprentice Reaper. The other two were women around the same age, though you couldn't really tell with Reapers. One was dark-skinned and dressed in a surprisingly skimpy purple outfit that revealed an array of tattoos on her shoulders and arms. The other girl, pale-skinned and blond, wore a neat smart-casual outfit more fitting of an intern than a Reaper and also wielded a scowl worthy of Cass on a bad day.

"You're Rory?" The dark-skinned woman offered me a smile. "I'm Alise. I'm Val's apprentice."

"Nice to meet you." When I turned to her companion, the blond woman's scowl deepened.

"Lara," she ground out. "I'm Freya's apprentice, and we both opposed a human being invited to our summit."

Friendly.

"And this is Reid," Alise said, indicating the young man. "He's new to the job. We're showing him the ropes."

"Yes, and we already have one person to babysit," Lara muttered in none-too-pleasant tones. "We don't need a human too."

"I don't need babysitting." The timid voice that came from her other target gave the opposite impression, but it did at least take her attention off me.

"Rory is here to introduce us to Ivory Beach. As a favour to me." A warning note entered Xavier's voice, and I felt a rush of gratitude. "Have any of you seen Evan?"

"He went into an empty room upstairs," said Lara in a bored voice. "Said he needed to study in silence."

"Study?" I asked. "For what, Reaper exams?"

Lara snorted. "He's just a swot. The real experience is out in the field, as everyone knows."

"Sure they do." Alise bounded to her feet. "He'll want to come and meet Rory. I'll fetch him. Which way were the stairs, again?"

"It'll be easier if I go and find him," Xavier said. "I'll be back in a minute."

He glided from the room, leaving me alone with the other Reaper apprentices. Both Lara and Reid avoided my gaze, but Alise seated herself next to me as soon as the door closed. "The Reapers didn't give you a hard time? I can't believe they dragged you in there to be questioned without even letting me say hello first. It's lucky my boss came to your rescue."

Lara scoffed. "This is why we shouldn't let humans in. They always need rescuing."

"Sounds like Rory is the one who did the rescuing," said Alise. "She even saved Xavier's life at least once."

"Maybe that says more about him than her," Lara said caustically. "Nothing is more lethal to a Reaper than falling in love with a human."

Ouch. Anger flickered inside me, but I forced myself to respond calmly. "Our relationship is none of your business."

I was used to the Grim Reaper taking cheap shots at my feelings for Xavier enough that a few snarky comments from an apprentice would barely sting under normal circumstances, but the grilling the Reapers had given me had left my nerves a tad sensitive, to say the least.

"That's right," said Alise. "Just because you had to dump *your* human boyfriend because your boss is an utter bore—"

"Xavier." Reid sat up in his seat. "Where's Evan?"

Xavier stood in the doorway, his face even paler than usual. "He's dead."

3

"Dead?" echoed Alise. "Are you sure?"

"Looks that way," Xavier said grimly. "It's hard to fake."

For a Reaper, that was certainly so. We all looked at one another uneasily for a long moment before Reid broke eye contact first. "We should make sure he is dead before we tell anyone."

"Wouldn't you have sensed his death?" I whispered to Xavier as we all left the room. "Wouldn't everyone else in the house have also sensed it, for that matter?"

"That's what I thought," he murmured back, "but we didn't. He's definitely dead, though—his soul has gone."

My heart lurched. How could a house full of Reapers not have sensed the demise of one of their own?

Xavier led the way up the creaky wooden staircase to the house's upper level. I'd rarely set foot upstairs during my other visits here, and like the downstairs floor, there were more rooms up here than two people could possibly use even if they hadn't been Reapers. Evan's body lay in the doorway to one of those rooms, half sprawled on the threshold, his pale eyes staring sightlessly at the ceiling and his lips slightly parted.

Nobody could have had any doubt that he was dead, yet it seemed impossible that no Reaper had sensed his departure. Xavier could sense any deaths that occurred on the other side of *town*, so how could Evan's demise not have caught his attention? Not to mention the Grim Reaper's much sharper senses and those of his visitors.

"He's gone." Lara's sneer had outright vanished, though she sharply elbowed me aside as she crouched down and extended her hands over the body. "Only a Reaper can have done this."

Alise gasped.

Reid whispered, "Are you saying someone in the house killed him?"

"There aren't a whole lot of other Reapers in town, are there?" Lara's scathing tone lacked any real malice. "We'd better tell Gwyn. He's not going to be happy."

"It's not usually him who loses his apprentice to unfortunate accidents," Alise added in an undertone. When Reid flinched again, she flashed him an apologetic look. "Just saying."

A chill breeze swept upstairs, prompting me to turn around. The other Reapers must have realised something was wrong, as they'd gathered at the foot of the stairs with the Grim Reaper at their lead.

"What are you all doing up there?" he asked of Xavier.

"It's Evan," Lara called downstairs. "He's dead."

"Dead?" Gwyn stepped to the forefront with his giant wolfhound by his side. "Don't be ridiculous. We would have sensed it."

"His soul… It's gone." Lara's voice sounded strangely quiet, and she shrank back when Evan's mentor came gliding upstairs with his wolfhound swift on his heels.

The rest of us hastily moved out of the way, too, while the other Reapers crowded around the body.

A tense prolonged pause ensued before the Grim Reaper spoke. "She's right. His soul has gone. Yet we did not sense his death."

"That means another Reaper was the killer," said Lara.

An ominous silence crystallised, and the atmosphere turned frosty enough that I half expected icicles to spring up on the ceiling and walls.

"Leave us," Gwyn growled. "I will examine my apprentice myself."

"This is my house," said the Grim Reaper. "It shall be I who examines him."

Oh boy. Sensing trouble brewing, Xavier took my arm, and by mutual assent, the apprentices and I retreated down the stairs and left the Reapers to argue it out over Evan's body.

When we reached the living room again, Alise gave a wry chuckle. "This is going well. They haven't even started the summit yet, and someone's dead."

"When did it happen?" Reid asked shakily, sinking into an armchair. "He went upstairs—what, half an hour before Xavier got back?"

"It must have happened when I was fetching Rory from the library," Xavier agreed.

"That gives you both an alibi," said Alise thoughtfully. "And all of us were in here, weren't we? None of us apprentices left this room after he went to study upstairs."

"You don't really think one of the *Reapers* killed him?" Reid said. "No... it must have been an accident."

"I suppose you'd know, given how many apprentices Janus has already lost," Lara added. "That, or Janus's current apprentice was trying to wipe out the competition."

Reid gave her an appalled look. "How would I reap his soul? I don't even have a scythe yet."

"Lara, if that was a joke, it wasn't a funny one." Alise's brow furrowed. "Hmm. Maybe it *was* Janus, and he decided to make the other Reapers go through the same thing he usually does out of spite."

"That doesn't even make sense," Lara said. "Besides, we're not the ones who are supposed to find the person responsible."

"It's Charon's house," said Alise. "That means it should be his job to investigate a death on his property. Though since Gwyn is the one who lost his apprentice, he might claim authority… This is going to get messy."

"He's also not impartial." Xavier paced across the room, his manner agitated. "I don't know that *anyone* is, to be honest. All the Reapers were in the house at the time, but that doesn't mean they can't have been responsible for his death."

"Not when any Reaper might have been able to hop upstairs via the afterworld and kill Evan without leaving the room for longer than a second," I concluded. "Oh. I see."

That was the problem. Reapers could pretty much be in two places at once, or as close as was possible in the magical world. All it'd take was one lapse in the others' attention, and they might not have known someone had slipped away to commit murder.

"That may be, but there's still the question of why nobody else sensed Evan's death," Xavier said. "That's the worrying part. Someone planned this carefully."

They did. "If we can't work out *how* they did it, we need to find out who doesn't have an alibi for his time of death," I said. "If we need someone impartial to question everyone, there's Edwin. He would want to know someone was murdered, even a Reaper."

"You know what my boss would say to that."

I did. Unfortunately.

"Who's Edwin?" asked Alise.

"Head of the local police department," I said. "He usually doesn't like people taking the law into their own hands, but he tends to make an exception for the Reapers."

"Maybe that's what we need." Alise raised her voice over the loud arguing outside the room. "It sounds like they need someone who's an impartial outsider. A non-Reaper."

All eyes turned to me.

"What?" I swivelled toward Xavier. "The Reapers would never let *me* get involved."

"Definitely not," he said firmly. "No, Alise, Rory is not going to help with the investigation."

"The other Reapers would be more likely to let Edwin talk to them." Or maybe not. "He's head of the police and has authority."

"He's also an outsider," said Xavier. "My boss wouldn't get past that part."

Was there anyone the Reapers *wouldn't* object to? That was debatable. None of them had been overly thrilled at my appearance, and I'd been here as a guest, not an investigator.

"Xavier." The Grim Reaper appeared in the doorway and beckoned to his apprentice. "I want to talk to you alone. You too, Aurora."

I took in a breath and followed him into the hallway. I could only assume I was about to get unceremoniously booted out of the house, but I forced myself to speak calmly. "What is it?"

"I find myself in a dilemma," he said. "Someone in this house is a murderer, and none will submit to me for questioning alone. They would only answer to an impartial outside party."

"But not an actual outsider?" I glanced at Xavier. "You

want him to do it? Because if Evan died while he was fetching me from the library, we were the only two people not inside the house when he was murdered."

"That does seem to be the case." He loomed over me, his shadowy face expressionless. I wished he'd put his hood down for once, but he must have been set on distinguishing himself from the other Reapers just by being the creepiest. "I am sure you know why you cannot share a word of this outside the house."

"Of course I do." *Wait a moment.* "Are you saying you want *me* to help with the questioning?"

"I said nothing of the sort."

Right. "Have you worked out *how* he died?"

A moment passed. "His soul has gone."

"Which doesn't explain how he died," I added. "If you can't tell by looking at him, it's not the worst idea to have someone else examine the body."

"Nobody can be trusted not to share the details with outsiders."

"What about Edwin? He—"

"Out of the question. The Reapers' secrets are not to be exposed to any humans, especially the death of one of our own."

I suppressed a groan. "Then what? Xavier can't sense how Evan died any more than you can. Even if you won't involve the authorities, any witch would be able to at least identify his death as having a magical cause." *Even me.* I didn't say the last part aloud, but Xavier glanced at me, my name on his lips.

"You would be able to verify the cause of death?" asked the Grim Reaper. "Are you truly so accomplished in your training as a witch?"

The scepticism in his tone was kind of uncalled for. It wasn't like he could use regular magic himself. "I never said I was an expert, but if you won't let anyone else into the house, someone has to do it."

"No." His tone held a sense of finality. "The questioning will take place first. I will verify the whereabouts of each Reaper at the time of the death and will extract a confession from whoever was responsible for Evan's fate. With the killer identified, there will be no need to have the body examined."

"And I'm to conduct the questioning?" Xavier guessed.

"Correct."

"Not alone." A rush of protectiveness seized me. Yes, Xavier dealt with the dead all the time, but a dead *Reaper* was another story. The incident was bound to have been a shock to him. Maybe if the questioning came to nothing, the Grim Reaper would rethink the merits of having someone else take a closer look at the body. "What if whoever did this wasn't working alone? If they were taking orders from—from someone else?"

Like one of the Founders? Yes, it would take more than a vampire's powers to cut off a Reaper's awareness of the afterworld, but the Founders *had* allied with a rogue Reaper, and more recently, they'd been working on potions designed to be used against Reapers. Who was to say what else they might have concocted?

"The Founders." Xavier had come to the same conclusion as me. "If there's vampire involvement—"

"I will not allow the leader of the vampires to have any knowledge of this incident," said the Grim Reaper with a warning note to his voice that seemed entirely directed at me.

"Knowing Evangeline, she'll figure it out on her own," said Xavier. "Rory won't tell anyone."

"I won't," I confirmed. "Evangeline is known for lurking around, spying on people, and a group of Reapers visiting town won't have escaped her attention. I bet she's already been watching the house."

"Exactly," said Xavier. "I don't like the idea of Rory being involved in this, but she's right. Wasn't the main subject of the discussions at the summit going to concern the Founders and their schemes against the Reapers?"

"Also, Xavier and I are the only people who weren't in the house at the time," I added. "If you must make him question everyone alone, at least let me sit in there for moral support. It won't involve me overhearing any Reaper secrets."

The Grim Reaper's shadowed gaze passed between us. "Then I will let you ask questions of each of my fellow Reapers. You will act as impartial observers, and you will not speak a word of this to anyone outside."

He actually said yes? I hadn't expected him to, but I'd felt compelled to volunteer for Xavier's sake.

Even Xavier himself looked taken aback. As his boss glided away, he turned to me. "Are you sure about this?"

"Definitely not, but someone has to do it."

"I honestly don't know where to start with this questioning," admitted Xavier. "How can anyone tell if a Reaper is lying? I can't, and I *live* with one."

"Well, there's one obvious candidate," I murmured. "The person who has a habit of losing his apprentices in accidents. I mean, it sounds like he has a reputation already."

"It wasn't Janus's apprentice who died, though." His expression darkened. "I don't know why he'd target Gwyn's apprentice rather than his own. They've rarely met."

"It's somewhere to start." I glanced toward the meeting room. "That is, if they even let us question them."

"They might object, but they'll know it's the right thing to do." Xavier took a decisive step. "Someone has to get answers, and they're not going to get anywhere by arguing amongst themselves."

Yeah, but if the Reapers can't figure it out, I'm hardly qualified. I'd been making fast progress in my witch lessons, but the kind of experimental magic the Founders dabbled in was generally unknown to anyone outside their ranks.

As I'd expected, the other Reapers weren't exactly taken with the news that a human would be helping with the questioning. When we entered, they immediately broke into loud objections.

"It's the only way to ensure the questioning is done by someone impartial who also won't share anything with outsiders," said Xavier. "Rory and I weren't at the house when Evan died, and we're sworn to secrecy."

"Sounds fair," Val said. "Hey! Quieten down, everyone. Would you rather be questioned by those two or by the entire Reaper Council?"

That shut them up. Gwyn turned baleful eyes upon Xavier and me. "What is your intention?"

"We'll question you one at a time," decided Xavier. "That way, we'll get everyone's account separately, and we can see if there are any contradictions."

"Best way to cover the tricky business of people hopping around the afterworld," Val agreed, shooting me a wink. "Bet this one would cause headaches for the police."

The other Reapers cast disapproving looks in her direction, but when Xavier called Janus to be questioned first, his companions obligingly rose to their feet and left the room.

The older Reaper's scowl reached astronomical proportions when he faced us at the head of the table. "This is unnecessary," he growled. "I was inside this room during the entire time that elapsed after the young apprentice went upstairs. The others can confirm that's true."

"Were they all inside the room for the whole of that time too?" I asked. "Did anyone disappear, even for a second?"

"Yes," he said. "Freya went outside for about twenty minutes shortly before the meeting started, and Val went to speak to her apprentice a moment later."

His claims matched up with the others', and I made a mental note to ask Val and Freya if anyone could verify whether they'd returned immediately to the meeting room without taking any other detours. That was assuming Janus told the truth, but Janus didn't have any noticeable red flags aside from his supposed history with apprentices meeting unfortunate fates, so we brought the interview to an end and called in the next Reaper.

Gwyn entered with his wolfhound in tow. I leaned back in my seat while the beast towered over the table with its shaggy paws placed on a chair. Gwyn answered all the questions in a monotone, claiming that he'd been in the room the whole time and that he would never have hurt his apprentice.

"Neither would Hunt," he growled when Xavier asked if his wolfhound shared the same alibi.

Good thinking, I thought. "Was he here the whole time as well?" Might the giant beast have sneaked through the afterworld behind his owner's back and killed his master's apprentice? That seemed unlikely, and it would probably have been obvious if the giant hound had vanished in the middle of the meeting.

"He was," Gwyn confirmed. "As the others can verify."

"The other apprentices said Evan was working on an assignment upstairs," I said, moving on to the next topic. "Was that true?"

"Yes," he said. "Training a new apprentice from scratch will be a significant setback."

It didn't sound like he was *too* heartbroken to lose his apprentice, but then again, Reapers' emotions were hard to read, and they spent so much time close to death that they didn't react to it in the same way. No other issues leapt at me, so it was time to move on.

Next up was Val, who sauntered confidently into the room as if she was at a hairdressers' appointment rather than an interrogation.

"You may have heard from the others that I went to talk to Alise for a couple of minutes earlier," she said. "I never went upstairs, though, and I didn't even notice Evan wasn't in the apprentices' room."

"Did any of the other apprentices see you return to the meeting room?"

"I guess not." She drummed her fingers on the table. "But Charon would have known I'd gone upstairs."

I'd have to take her word for it on that, but I had a hard time seeing her as the killer. Not only was her attitude all wrong, but she had no motive that I knew of.

That left just Freya to question, and when Gwyn departed, she entered the room in the manner of a teacher arriving to rain hellfire upon a disobedient pupil. She did not sit down, instead standing at the head of the table with a glare strong enough to level a mountain.

"We'd like you to explain where you were at the time of Evan's death," I said, trying to keep my nerves under control. "Were you here in this room the whole time?"

"No," she replied haughtily. "I went outside to make a phone call."

"Did anyone see you leave?"

"No, but I shouldn't have to justify myself to a human," she said. "Unless you have a plan to become an apprentice yourself, you have no business being here."

"Rory has a right to be here," Xavier said. "She's helped the Reapers enough times."

"Reapers shouldn't need help from any humans," she said. "It's an insult to all of us when you share our secrets with outsiders and allow them to be privy to information that even apprentices must gain a level of trust before being allowed to access. To say nothing of the cruelty you're inflicting on her yourself by offering her such false hopes."

"False hopes?" I echoed, confused.

She gave me a look of pure disdain. "Hope that you can maintain a relationship with a Reaper. It's out of the question. He's immortal. You're mortal, and one day, it might be *your* soul he has to remove from this world."

My heart dropped like a stone, and all the words died in my throat.

"That's enough," Xavier said. "Rory made her choice, and so did I."

"Is she going to be an apprentice, then?" said Freya. "I doubt it. She'll have to give up that family of hers, and from what I can tell, she isn't willing to do that. Reapers can't have it both ways. You should know that yourself, Xavier."

My heart continued to sink until it took up residence somewhere in the Earth's core.

Xavier glared at her, and a shiver trailed down my spine when shadows crept around his edges, making him look more of a Reaper than I'd ever seen him. "My relationship with Rory is irrelevant to this murder. So far, you're the only person without an alibi, so I will tell my supervisor to act accordingly."

Luckily, the Grim Reaper chose that moment to make an appearance, gliding into the room and addressing the pair of us. "I think that concludes the questioning. You may leave."

What, leave the room or the house? I assumed the latter, and frankly, part of me wanted to go back to the library and curl up in a corner with a book to rid myself of the sting of

Freya's words. But however cutting her remarks might have been, that didn't make them true.

Someone was dead. That was more important than Freya's irrational grudge, and I might have to face much worse than her barbed words to find out the truth.

4

The three remaining apprentices watched Xavier and me enter the room with open curiosity. He'd given me the option to walk home and decompress after we spoke to the other Reapers, but I didn't have much enthusiasm for the idea of answering the inevitable deluge of questions from my family members, and Aunt Candace's request for a full report might expand even further when she found out someone was dead.

Besides, the Reapers might not be the only ones keeping secrets. Their apprentices might too.

My certainty rapidly trickled away when Lara's cutting eyes followed me across the room as I joined Xavier on the sofa. Her attitude toward me was plainly a product of her mentor's, and if Freya's sharp comments had been an attempt to shut down my questions, I could deal with anything her apprentice threw at me too.

"So," said Alise. "How'd it go?"

"What kind of question is that?" Lara tapped her fingers irritably on the cover of a notebook she had open in her lap.

Studying, was she? "It's a waste of time, if you ask me. Nobody is going to confess anything to a human."

"So you think someone in there *does* have a confession to make?" Alise's voice brimmed with curiosity. "This has to be a first."

Lara's eyes narrowed in answer. I watched her, a question stirring on my tongue. *Was it your mentor?* I knew asking that question would lead nowhere good, but while Xavier and I hadn't actively been asked to question the other apprentices, they *were* technically witnesses who could back up their mentors' alibis.

I started with Alise. "Did your mentor come to check on you just before Xavier and I showed up at the house?"

"Sure," she said. "Why?"

"It's the only time she was out of the room," I explained. "The Grim Reaper would want to confirm her story, but it sounds like she was only gone a moment."

Lara rolled her eyes. "Now you're interrogating us? Are you hoping that solving this murder will win you more privileges with the Reapers?"

A spate of recklessness seized me. "And *your* mentor was missing for almost the entire window in which Evan was killed."

A faint flush coloured Lara's pale face. "You're accusing my mentor?"

"I didn't accuse her, I just asked what she was doing alone outside at the time of the murder," I said. "She didn't give Xavier and me much of an alibi."

"I hardly think it's your business."

"We were assigned to question the Reapers as outside observers," said Xavier. "It's that or bring in a proper interrogator, and I think my mentor would prefer to avoid drawing the attention of the Reaper Council just yet."

Lara flushed even more, while Reid's eyes darted around

as if he wanted to flee into the afterworld to get away from the brewing tension. Xavier was right, though. We didn't need a whole group of other Reapers descending on town right before Christmas. This current group was trouble enough on their own.

If Freya *had* been roaming around the house for the purpose of killing another apprentice—however odd that might seem—would Lara have covered for her? Quite possibly yes, but I could say the same for Alise and *her* mentor.

As for Reid, his nervousness wasn't a red flag on its own, but Lara's remark about him targeting the competition came to mind. The accusation had sounded vaguely ridiculous, but his own mentor's history raised a fair few questions about how he treated his apprentices. Reid himself had said he hadn't got his own scythe yet, and removing someone's soul was a tall order without any Reaper instrument to do so with.

"Hey, I'm happy to answer any questions," Alise said. "I know the others saw Val come in too... so, Lara, what *was* your mentor doing outside?"

"You're taking this seriously?" said Lara. "Really, it's more likely to be an outsider who did it, someone who wanted to frame one of us."

"Who can feign a death inflicted by a Reaper?" I expected another eye roll in return, but an uneasy moment of silence passed across all the apprentices.

Not only had Evan's soul been taken, but nobody in the house had sensed it, and that alone pointed to a cause that might lie outside the Reapers' sphere of knowledge—and mine too.

The sound of raised voices from the meeting room prompted Xavier to move closer to the door. "I think we should leave. They'll be at it for a while, and besides, we haven't given you the tour of Ivory Beach yet. What do you think, Rory?"

"Isn't it still raining?" *Not that that would be a deterrent to anyone in here except for me.*

"No, it stopped," he said. "We can do the tour another time, but I just figured it would be more interesting than staying in here all day while they argue."

"I, for one, couldn't care less," said Lara. "I don't need to see any more of this dismal place."

"I do," said Alise. "I haven't seen the sea in months."

I couldn't possibly have felt *less* like being a tour guide, but staying in this freezing house with a dead body was unappealing at best.

When we were halfway to the door, the Grim Reaper called Xavier back into the meeting room.

"Now?" Xavier cast me an apologetic look. "I have to go in. I'll try to join you later."

"What's he want this time?" Alise pushed open the front door. "Let's not let them ruin the fun, Rory. C'mon."

Xavier's departure left me in the reluctant role of tour guide. While the cemetery was still drenched in rainwater and the air was icy cold, the breeze was also somewhat refreshing after the stuffiness of the Grim Reaper's living room, and Alise's enthusiasm had her racing out into the high street right away.

I followed, humouring her as she ducked in and out of shops and admired the vibrant displays in the windows. While she was busy fawning over a life-size reindeer designed to take a small child for a ride, I was left on the sidelines with Reid.

"How long have you been training as a Reaper?" I asked him, mostly to take my mind off the cold wind trying to creep inside my coat.

"Three months," he replied. "I didn't know Evan, but I'm sorry he's dead. Gwyn is a decent boss from what I've heard."

"What about Janus?" I asked delicately. "I mean, it's fine if you don't want to tell me. I know non-Reapers aren't supposed to ask that kind of question."

"Ignore Lara," he said, to my surprise. "Most of us don't hold *that* tightly to the rules. It wasn't that long ago that we were regular humans, after all."

How long? It wasn't a question I'd ever asked Xavier—the *no aging* thing kind of made things like that irrelevant—but it had always been lodged in the back of my mind. And Freya's caustic remarks had been a sharp reminder that I didn't know nearly as much about the Reapers' process of inducting their apprentices as I'd thought. For instance, the others had all but certainly picked being a Reaper over their human families. Xavier might not have had one, but what of the others?

"Yeah." I dragged my thoughts away from that morbid path. "Xavier hasn't had a problem with bringing me on board, especially as we've dealt with threats that affect the Reapers too."

His pace slowed, his eyes widening a little. "The vampires, right? I heard something Xavier said... He mentioned the Founders."

"Yes." How much had Xavier told the others? He'd given a full report to the other Reapers, I had no doubt, but I wasn't sure about their apprentices. Then again, most of the information was public, at least to those of us who'd been involved. "All the Founders we're aware of are currently in jail, though."

That didn't mean they hadn't been the instigators of this, but I didn't need the others to end up drawing their own conclusions. I wasn't supposed to play detective on my own either.

"Good," he said. "I don't know too much about them, but my boss sticks to a rigid curriculum. He says I don't need to be distracted by Council business just yet."

"I didn't know there was a curriculum for Reapers."

"A loose one," he replied, "since some Reapers get more training than others, over different time spans. It depends how young they're taken in. Xavier is probably further along than most of us since he was pretty much born into the role."

"You signed up later?"

"Yes, but it's usually not until we're full-grown adults that we're actually inducted as apprentices and start serious training," he clarified, "since that's the point at which we stop ageing. Nobody wants a Reaper to eternally look like a teenager. We aren't like the vampires."

I suppressed a flinch of horror. *Oh.* I hadn't even thought of that, but it made a horrible kind of sense. It also meant Xavier had grown up as any human would have until he stepped over the invisible line to Reaperhood and left his humanity behind.

"It can vary, though," he added. "Xavier knows more than I do since I'm still fairly new to this. Essentially, an apprentice has a full Reaper's advantages but not all the knowledge, and even then, it's no guarantee they'll qualify at the end of the process."

Or they'll survive it. I could fill in the blanks easily enough, and curiosity momentarily drove me to ask, "Why'd you do it, anyway? You knew what happened to the others, didn't you?"

His gaze dropped to his feet. "I heard the rumours, but I wanted to train as a Reaper."

"Seems a strange choice," I couldn't help saying. "I mean, if you weren't born into it. I can't imagine every kid wants to be the Reaper when they grow up. Not when they find out what it actually entails."

"I..." He shifted on his feet, looking self-conscious. "Someone I know was a Reaper, and I'm sure Lara or her boss already told you how it works if you love someone who —who isn't human."

I stiffened. "You loved someone who was a Reaper?"

"She's still a Reaper," he corrected. "She moved away from town when she was promoted from apprentice to full Reaper. There only needs to be one Reaper per region, and we already had one."

I turned this over in my head. "Janus? She was Janus's apprentice first? I thought the apprentice was supposed to take the mentor's place."

"Usually, that's how it goes, but there was a region where the Reaper, ah... retired early." He fidgeted with his sleeve, looking uncomfortable. "They needed someone to step in, and she volunteered."

"I didn't know retirement was an option."

Another shuffle of his feet. "It's not, really. Occasionally, a Reaper steps back from the role, but usually, it's a more permanent retirement."

"They die." *Way to overlook the obvious, Rory.* "It can't be that common, can it?"

I knew Reapers *could* die—the unfortunate fates of his predecessors proved that—but they were more resilient even than vampires in most aspects.

"It's rare," he confirmed. "And it's also rare for someone to be born into the job, simply because Reapers aren't allowed to have children. All three of us chose to opt in. Even Evan. And Alise... Ah, we should probably catch her up."

Sure enough, while we'd been talking, Alise had taken off up the high street with the enthusiasm of a dog left to roam freely in a park. I hastened to catch up with her before she reached the vampires' manor at the top and encouraged her to come down to the square instead.

Alise and Reid were suitably impressed with the library. "I'll take you on a tour later this week," I told them. "We're closed today due to the party last night."

"I'm sad I missed that," said Alise. "I haven't been to a party in years. Which way is the seafront?"

"That way."

She'd already taken off past the clock tower before I finished speaking, and while Reid could easily have matched her speed, he stuck with my normal human pace instead.

"I hope I didn't upset you," he said to me in an undertone. "You're young. You still have a long life ahead of you, and so does Xavier, I expect. Relatively speaking, I mean. He's still going to take his boss's place, but it won't be for a while."

If anything, that made me feel worse. Reid had loved a Reaper too, and it sounded as if the Reapers had not been willing to accommodate their relationship unless he became one of them.

If nothing else, I'd all but confirmed Reid wasn't the killer. He'd given up everything to be with the person he loved. Why jeopardise his chances by an act as irrational as killing another apprentice?

Forget it, Rory, I told myself firmly and followed Alise's path to the seafront. She insisted on buying ice cream from a bemused vendor at the local corner shop and skipped along the pier, eating it.

When I saw Xavier gliding toward us at speed, my insides twisted in a combination of relief and inexplicable dread.

"Your boss let you go?" I asked.

"Only on the condition that I stop Alise from going for a swim."

"I don't think she's in any danger of catching hypothermia." But she was certainly teetering close to the pier's edge. "Also, I don't think we should take them near the vampires' place."

"Definitely not," he said firmly. "When we're done here, I can walk you back to the library."

"Sounds good." I wouldn't be able to show them the inside of the library just yet, but I'd left my family to deal with cleaning up the aftermath of the party for long enough.

"I hope you're all right," Xavier murmured as we fell into step with one another. "I didn't want to put you in charge of running a tour so soon after the questioning, but I hoped it would help take your mind off everything."

I wished I could say it had worked, but I'd known what I risked when I started asking Reid questions. "Have the others stopped arguing yet?"

"Unfortunately not, but they agree that Freya is the one person without a solid alibi. That's why she snapped at you, Rory. She knows she might be in trouble."

"It's fine." It was not fine. My head was a whirlwind of conflicted thoughts, courtesy of Reid's revelations and the grim knowledge that he'd been in the same position as Xavier and I had not so long before. "Does your boss definitely think one of the other Reapers did it?" I asked, mostly so that he didn't realise anything was wrong.

"Almost certainly." A few raindrops began to fall. "You should get back to the library before it gets worse."

I couldn't summon up much conversation between the seafront and the library. The others went back to the cemetery while Xavier dropped me off on the doorstep, and I hugged him goodbye as if he was nothing but a normal human who'd taken me out on a date, not someone with whom I might not have a future at all, or at least a future that went beyond the next few years.

That Xavier would one day take his boss's place as a full Reaper and would be forced to leave me behind whether I joined him as a Reaper or not—I'd been trying to forget those inevitable facts, but I found myself yearning for a reassurance that not even Xavier himself could offer.

Naturally, as soon as I entered the library, Aunt Candace pounced on me. "Tell me everything."

I stepped away from her eager stare. "I'm really not in the mood."

"Trouble in paradise?" she said. "Or did that Reaper bring his friends to gang up on you? Want me to put a curse on them?"

"Someone *died*," I said before I could question the wisdom of telling her that. "One of the apprentices."

"What?" Estelle came up behind her, her arms full of leather-bound tomes. "Someone was killed? Really?"

"Murdered," I replied. "Please, none of you tell anyone else. Or write it into a book. That means you, Aunt Candace."

"Tch," said Aunt Candace. "So who do you think did it?"

"No clue," I replied. "It happened when Xavier was picking me up from the library, so we weren't in the house."

"Oh, one of the other *Reapers* is the killer?" Her notebook and pen nearly hit me in the back of the head as they bounced up and down in tandem with her excitement.

"Drop it, Aunt Candace," Estelle said. "If you're free to hound Rory, can you at least help me clean up down here?"

"I'll help." I pulled out my own wand and followed her through the lobby to the back, where the shelves around the Reading Corner had moved to form what appeared to be a giant shield. "What's this?"

"The library was trying to protect the Reading Corner from the party, I think, but now the shelves won't move back," Estelle explained.

"Ah." I lifted my wand, and Aunt Candace did too.

Clearly, she intended to stick around and hear an explanation even if it meant having to help out.

Aunt Adelaide made an appearance halfway through my

account of the murder, having been rearranging shelves up on the first floor that had been disturbed by the party.

"They're sure a Reaper did it?" Estelle asked anxiously when I'd finished. She and her mother exchanged worried looks. "I suppose that's better than the alternative."

"I'd say that awful Freya character did it," Aunt Candace said. "Or her apprentice."

"I'm inclined to believe the same," I admitted, "but a bad attitude doesn't make someone a killer."

"The one who usually loses his apprentices—what's his name, Janus?" said Estelle. "That sounds suspicious to me."

"That would be too obvious," Aunt Candace said with confidence. "No, I think I shall question them myself."

"You definitely won't," I said. "I probably won't be allowed to go back there myself, come to that."

"Well, that won't do, will it?"

"Candace, that's enough," said Aunt Adelaide. "We don't need either of you to risk your lives. It's already dangerous to the whole town if this killer remains uncaught."

"Then the Reapers need all the help they can get, I'd say," said Aunt Candace.

"Absolutely not." Cass popped up from behind a shelf, eyes narrowed behind her glasses and her red hair pulled into a messy bun as it usually was when she was with her animals. "You shouldn't have gone there at all, Rory. Now they're done with you, that should be the end of your involvement."

"Not necessarily," I said. "I don't *want* to be involved, but your mum's right. The town's at the centre of this, and we don't need the Reaper Council showing up on Christmas Eve."

"Some of us would greatly enjoy that," said Aunt Candace, who wore a Cheshire cat–like grin on her face. "Maybe you should sit this one out after all."

"There's also…" Estelle raised her voice over her mother's counterargument and Cass's sigh. "If it wasn't a Reaper, there's only one group who's come close to getting the better of them, right?"

"The Founders." Recently, they'd created a potion that could put Reapers to sleep, which was supposed to be impossible.

Had they also created a way to kill someone who was, by all definitions, already dead?

5

I was glad the library was closed for the rest of the day, as dealing with customers would have been a tough call, let alone with the appropriate level of cheer befitting the season. Why had the Reapers chosen *now* to host their summit and not a dismal weekday in the middle of January instead? It was hard to imagine Santa and his reindeer descending on the town when my mind was full of images of a troupe of Reaper Council members swooping down and handing out doom and fear instead of presents.

While my family and I returned the Reading Corner to its former state, they offered the occasional theory about who might be responsible for the murder. If the Reapers didn't want my involvement, they certainly wouldn't appreciate me dragging my family members along, whether it turned out the Founders had been involved in the death or otherwise. But the fact that the Grim Reaper had refused to let anyone else examine the body was a sticking point.

"It'll save time if they just let me do it," said Aunt Candace, who'd spent the past half hour throwing out increasingly absurd theories about what magical potions and curses might have led to Evan's death. "The disillusion draft would certainly require expert examination."

"Isn't that the one that turns someone's body inside out?" Estelle said from behind a nearby shelf, where Spark the pixie was trying unsuccessfully to lift a heavy hardcover book. "I think that the Reapers would have noticed if that's what happened to their apprentice."

"Definitely." I grimaced at the mental image. "If it *was* a potion, it was one that left no obvious marks that I could see. And, Aunt Candace, I told you: they won't let you in."

"They need an expert on potions," she said. "I can guarantee that once they have the cause of death pinned down, the killer's confession will practically write itself.'

"This isn't a book, Aunt Candace," I said. "Frankly, any sane person would want to *avoid* getting entangled in investigating a Reaper's murder."

"Your fatal mistake was believing me to be sane."

I snorted. At least her being downstairs meant that Jet, my familiar, had come out of her room, since the little crow spent most of his time following my aunt around, listening for gossip for her to use in her books. While his chatter was usually not what I needed when I was in a bad mood, it did cheer me up a little to have him sitting on a shelf, supervising our attempts to move the Reading Corner back where it was supposed to be.

When we cleared the path into the cosy area between the shelves, he followed me in, watching me with his beady little eyes.

"Don't be sad, partner!" he squeaked. "I'll go and spy on the Reapers and tell you what they're saying."

"Please don't."

My familiar was surprisingly good at lurking out of sight

when he wasn't talking at a mile a minute, but I definitely didn't want him hanging around outside the Reaper's house. Besides, there was no point. There was nothing I needed to hear in their discussions unless the killer made an unlikely confession in front of witnesses, which I sincerely doubted. Xavier would let me know if I was needed.

Instead, I had the afternoon free, so I decided to fish out a book to read so I could take my mind thoroughly off the situation with the Reapers. With the Reading Corner clear, I planted myself on a beanbag and reached into my bag for my current reads.

Instead, my hand closed on my dad's journal. Though I'd mostly translated its contents, I liked to flip back through and find new sections I'd missed in the interim. That happened a lot because Dad's journal was possibly the most disorganised document I'd ever encountered. Not only were the entries often written in the wrong order, but Dad had frequently gone back to previous entries and added comments and digressions in the margins that were even harder to read than the regular entries. Not to mention, the whole thing had been written in code when I found it, and while I'd eventually found a way to translate the code, courtesy of the magical Spell Assistant, the journal's piecemeal style meant I frequently missed things.

As I was turning pages, trying to find parts I'd accidentally skipped, Estelle entered the Reading Corner. "Are you all right?"

I lifted my head. "I was curious if my dad ever met the Reapers after the journal ends. It stops over twenty years ago."

The abrupt end suggested he'd run out of space. Maybe he'd also run out of things to write down, but I'd never thought to ask back when he was alive. While I'd known he kept a journal throughout my childhood, it had always been an object of vague curiosity he kept in the bookshelf and nothing remarkable on its own. As far as I could tell, the entries covered a span of time around when I was a baby up until I was around five or so.

When I first discovered the journal, it had been a revelation to know that Dad had had a whole secret life he'd never told me about. He'd left the library behind when he married my mother, since bringing normals into the magical world was strictly forbidden, but he'd never quite managed to get rid of his fascination with rare magical books.

"I didn't know you'd reached the end at all," Estelle said.

"Didn't you?" I showed her the last page. "It's not really an ending. It kinda doubles back on itself, and Dad starts writing random asides in the margins of previous entries. There are sections in the middle I haven't got to yet, for that reason."

"And you think he might have met the Grim Reaper again?"

"It's not really relevant, I know." I flipped back a few pages and was briefly caught by a digression that I thought mentioned the word *Reapers* but actually referred to a self-reading book. "I should be looking at more about his encounters with the Founders, but there aren't that many entries where they're mentioned directly."

It had been through his fascination with rare books that Dad became inadvertently tangled up with a group of vampires who shared that fascination for more sinister reasons. And when they found out he was keeping a journal, they'd wanted to get their hands on it.

"It might be," she said. "The Grim Reaper has a history that goes far beyond ours. They all do. Really, it's probably for the best if we leave them to deal with this themselves."

"I know," I said. "They made it clear they don't want me to

have anything to do with this, but I was already involved, and so was my dad."

My dad and the Grim Reaper had all but certainly met more than once, but since the journal stopped so abruptly, I didn't know if those meetings had continued after it had ended.

"Oh, Rory." She sat down next to me. "The apprentices were nice to you, right?"

"Except one." I pulled a face. "That's the problem, actually. Reid, one of the apprentices I spoke to, told me he signed up because he was in love with a Reaper. Let's just say it didn't work out well for them."

She sucked in a breath. "He fell in love with a Reaper? Surely that's allowed if they're both Reapers, right?"

"No relationships allowed." I blinked the sting from my eyes. "I knew that from the start, but I guess I've never heard it directly from someone else who used to be in the same position as we are."

"It's not the same, though," she said. "Not like you and Xavier. He fell in love with a full Reaper, not an apprentice, right?"

"She used to be an apprentice," I murmured, regretting bringing up the subject. "Then she qualified as a full Reaper and moved away from town. The point is, when Xavier takes his boss's place for good, I'll... I'll lose him." A lump grew in my throat.

"Oh, Rory." She hugged me. "Ignore them. You aren't in the same position as he was, and nobody else gets a say in your relationship. His boss gave you permission to be together no matter what the others think. That's enough, and he's not going to retire for a long while, is he?"

"I know." I half laughed. "That's the ridiculous part. The guy is immortal. We're talking vampire lifespans, not human ones."

That was another issue in itself, but I couldn't even go there right then.

Wiping my eyes, I turned back to the journal. "Anyway, my dad met the Grim Reaper at least once, and I guess I was wondering if they ever met up again and where."

"Or if anyone else in our family did the same." A thoughtful expression came over her. "They *might* have. We've owned this library for generations, since long before Grandma turned it into what it is now."

"Good point." Grandma had made the library semisentient, but my family's biblio-witch magic went back countless generations, and our ancestors had always been heavily involved in collecting rare books. My current family members' knowledge, like mine, was stymied by Grandma inconveniently taking all her secrets with her to her grave—or locking them up on the fourth floor.

"What is it?" Estelle asked when I got to my feet.

"The fourth floor." I half sat down again. "I was just thinking that it's a shame there isn't a wish that will grant us access to all Grandma's secrets and Dad's too. But Dad wasn't living here when he wrote this." I gestured to the journal.

"True, and I bet the Grim Reaper told him not to write anything down."

"If he did, my dad didn't listen." But he'd stopped writing in his journal long before his death, and I didn't know what he did next.

"I guess it's a family habit." A smile came to her mouth. "I know this is weighing on you, Rory, but you did nothing wrong. The Reapers' issues with humans are their problem, not yours."

"It wasn't a human who murdered one of them." I took in a breath. "It was either a Reaper or someone equally powerful. Like… the vampires."

"You think they were involved? The Founders?"

"There's no proof," I said. "Removing someone's soul… There are ways to do it without involving a Reaper, but he *was* killed inside a Reaper's house, and they'd know if someone else had sneaked in. And there's the fact that none of the Reapers sensed his death either."

"Hmm." She looked contemplative. "Would the Book of Questions have any ideas?"

"Absolutely not." The firm voice came from Sylvester, who'd flown silently down from the top of his tree at some point during our conversation and perched on a bookshelf to listen in.

"I wasn't going to ask you," I informed him, "so you can stop eavesdropping on us now."

"It's my business if you're thinking of doing something unwise that will endanger the library as well as yourself," he said, "and inserting yourself into the Reapers' business is a very good way to do that."

"This is hardly the first time," I protested. "Anyway, a Reaper being murdered is the sort of incident that draws attention even if the library isn't directly involved. If the Reapers can't solve this among themselves, the Reaper Council will descend on Ivory Beach. None of us wants that."

He gave a disapproving hoot and lifted his tawny wings. "We most certainly do not, but the Reapers are not detectives, and neither are you."

"You don't have to remind me," I muttered. "Unless you think I should call the police? You think the Grim Reaper would go for that?"

"No," he answered.

"Then give me answers or go away." I shooed him away half-heartedly.

He responded by spreading his wings even wider until he cast a giant owl-shaped shadow over my head. "I don't have the answers, but I do have a firm warning against surrendering your humanity to the masters of death."

"Huh?" I blinked at him. "You're giving me advice against joining the Reapers?"

"Most people wouldn't need that advice." He clucked his beak. "You don't want to leave your mortal life behind, do you?"

"No, I don't, and it's not your business if I did." I rubbed my forehead, a headache brewing. "Drop it, Sylvester. I don't need to hear—"

"Intruder!" The owl let out such a shriek that my eardrums screamed in protest, and the Christmas tree shuddered when he broke into a low dive that had me tripping over my own feet to get out of the way.

Then I saw who'd drawn his attention: Evangeline, the leader of the vampires. As eerily beautiful as usual, she wore a smile that showed she was completely unperturbed by the furious owl hovering above with his talons inches from her glossy black hair.

"Now, this isn't a very nice welcome, Aurora, is it?" she said in sickly sweet tones.

"We're closed," I said. "Sylvester is asking you nicely to leave."

"I cannot do that, Aurora," she said. "I must speak with you of a subject with great urgency."

"Meaning what?" I knew what: the Reapers. She knew about the murder, but did she have any idea who was responsible?

"I was surprised this town was volunteered to host the Reapers' summit," she said. "Recent events aside, I had some concerns about certain individuals among their little group, but I trusted that our own Grim Reaper knew best. Charon, it seems, chose wrongly."

"One of the Reapers?" I guessed. "What concerns, exactly?

Do you have a history with others, like you do with the Grim Reaper?" Of course *she'd* known his real name and probably a lot more besides.

"I said nothing of the sort."

"That means yes." Why she couldn't just give me a straight answer was one of the reasons I hadn't considered speaking to her beforehand, at least without any obvious link connecting this murder to the vampires. "You came here to bother me for a reason, right? I assume it's because you know I was asked to help with questioning the suspects in Evan's death, so I'd appreciate it if you were honest with me."

"I have not told you any lies," she said. "I came here as a favour and to warn you. Do not trust the other Reapers."

"I never did." I frowned in suspicion. "Do you know who the murderer is? If so, please say it. Or tell the Grim Reaper or his apprentice. I'm sure he'd rather know before he has to invite the Reaper Council to town to clear it up."

"I have no knowledge of the person responsible for the recent tragic death of a Reaper's apprentice, Aurora," she said. "All Reapers' minds are locked to me, and I can only make guesses.

Right. She couldn't read their minds, but that didn't mean she knew nothing of their potential motives. "Even a guess is better than what we've got. Do... Do you think the Founders are involved?"

"I couldn't possibly say," she said blandly. "I am not allowed to enter the Reapers' home myself, you remember, and I only know what I've been able to discern from the circumstances. A Reaper dead, and the others none the wiser as to the culprit."

Does she know the Reapers didn't sense Evan's death? If not, I didn't really want to enlighten her. She clearly disliked being out of the loop, but any proof of the Founders' involvement would bring worse than the Reaper Council upon Ivory Beach.

"More or less, but he wasn't bitten by a vampire as far as I know." *Not that I'd thought to check.* "It's not going to endear me to them if I walk in there and tell them that you dropped some vague hints that you have all the answers but refused to give any details."

"I am not the right person to speak to them, Aurora, and I have no intention of drawing the ire of the Reapers' summit," she said. "A few questions on your part will get to the truth of the matter."

"So you think it's okay if *I* make them mad at me?" *As if I haven't already done that just by daring to walk in there and question them at all?* "They won't believe me without proof."

Evangeline gave me a probing stare that brought the creeping suspicion that I'd accidentally let a few stray unwanted thoughts creep out of the barrier I'd been practising conjuring around my mind to keep her out. But all she said was, "That is your choice, Aurora."

In a blink, she was gone. Sylvester hooted again in disapproval but didn't follow her. Given the sheer speed at which vampires could move, she might well be halfway across town before I could reach the door.

Dammit.

"Seriously?" I said to nobody in particular. "She wants me to barge into the Reapers' meeting room and start asking more questions until I unearth a connection to the Founders?"

"I would have thought you'd be keen to seize on the excuse to go back there," said the owl.

"No way," I said, only half truthful. "She didn't give me any *proof* the Founders were involved, and the Grim Reaper isn't going to change his tune due to a hunch on behalf of the head vampire. Anyway, Sylvester, I would have thought you'd be clamouring to stop me from running back to the Reapers and endangering the library in the process. Isn't that exactly what you were trying to warn me about?"

"I rather expect you made up your mind the instant that dead body showed up," was his response. "Do try to refrain from ending up in the same position yourself, won't you?"

6

Sylvester took flight before I could answer, at which point Aunt Adelaide came hurrying into view. "Rory, was that Evangeline?"

"Yes." My heart gave a belated stutter. "I think she just told me to warn the Reapers that one of their group is playing for the wrong side."

Unless I misread her words, and the cryptic nature of her warning left a lot of room for misinterpretation. But given the undoubted danger of being inside the same house as a killer, I had to at least try to warn Xavier.

The universe had other ideas. I fished my phone out of my pocket and sent a message that promptly bounced back with an error message attached: "No signal."

That was nothing new, given that both the library and the cemetery tended to scramble both phone and internet connections, and the presence of so many Reapers was bound to dampen any technology in the area.

"I'm sure he's okay," Aunt Adelaide reassured me. "The Grim Reaper will be watching the situation carefully, and it's unlikely that the killer will be able to escape his attention long enough to hurt anyone else."

"I know he's probably still interrogating the others," I acknowledged, "but if there's something Evangeline knows and even *he* doesn't, someone needs to enlighten him."

Preferably before any more victims are claimed.

If someone in that house did have a history with the vampires—with the Founders—the only members of that group within reach were imprisoned in the dungeon of Evangeline's home. While she'd given no hint that any of them had had a taste of freedom anytime recently, they were the sole source of possible information in town on the immortal collectors who'd plagued me since my arrival in the magical world.

But the last time I'd set foot in that dungeon, Laney had ended up in a coma and had nearly died.

Aunt Adelaide drew in a breath. "You should take someone else with you."

"Jet will come with me," I decided. "The Grim Reaper will already be looking for a reason to throw me out. I don't need to let him know I've told the whole family about this Reaper's death."

"I'll come with you, partner!" Jet squeaked enthusiastically, landing on my shoulder.

Aunt Adelaide's expression clouded. "I don't like this, but if you're sure, you'd better go before it's dark."

Estelle agreed with her mother, and I ducked outside before Aunt Candace could ambush me again or Sylvester could raise another objection. That he seemed to have got it into his head that I *wanted* to sign up as a Reaper apprentice was baffling, but it was often hard to tell if the owl was being serious or just winding me up.

Once outside, Jet flew alongside me and kept up a stream of chattering that didn't quite erase my rattled nerves. When

I got to the cemetery, I directed him to wait outside while I rang the doorbell. To my intense relief, it was Xavier who answered the door.

"Rory." His brow creased. "What is it?"

I took in a breath. "I couldn't get through to you on the phone and I… thought you should know. Evangeline showed up in the library."

His brows shot up. "She knows?"

"Of course she does. She's probably been spying on you the whole time."

His expression darkened. "What did she say? Come in, it's freezing out there."

I entered and did my best not to drip too much rainwater on the Grim Reaper's floor as I told Xavier in a whisper about the vampires' leader's unexpected visit.

"That's bad news," he murmured. "If one of the Reapers has been involved with the Founders… But I wouldn't have thought my boss would invite them into the house if they had, and I find it hard to believe he didn't know."

"Me too," I said, "but would Evangeline have shown up at the library if she didn't believe what she told me?"

His shoulders tensed. "Did she give any clues about who it was? Which Reaper?"

"Unfortunately not," I said. "She was vague as she always is, and then she ran off before I could ask her more in-depth questions. My only other idea was to ask her prisoners since they're the only people in town who might have had recent contact with the Founders, but Evangeline seemed pretty insistent that I had to get the truth out of whichever Reaper she was talking about."

"Damn." He glanced over his shoulder. "All right, I'll tell my boss."

He hadn't taken two steps before the Grim Reaper came drifting through the closed meeting room door and levelled me with the kind of stare that shouldn't have been possible for someone whose hood covered his entire face.

"What exactly are you doing here, Aurora?" he asked.

"Evangeline showed up at the library and said that one of the Reapers here had a history with the vampires," I whispered. "She didn't specify which Reaper, but I thought you should know."

A shiver sprang to my arms as the Grim Reaper's shadow seemed to thicken around the edges, as if the afterworld itself was woven into his cloak. Rather than pulling his scythe on me, however, he pushed open the meeting room door.

I took a step back. "What are you doing?" I hissed. "I can't go in there. Nobody is going to confess to me."

The Grim Reaper glided into the room. The message was clear: I had to make the accusation myself or not at all.

"I'll do it." Xavier walked into the room, and I hurried in behind him before I lost my nerve.

The four Reapers stopped midargument to watch us enter with escalating levels of disdain, with the exception of Val, who wore an expression of mild amusement at the whole situation.

Xavier and I strode to the unoccupied seats at the long table, and he addressed the others with his usual clear calmness. "We've been made aware that one of you has been involved with the vampires in the past. Would anyone like to make a confession?"

An ominous silence descended on the table. Val arched a brow, her smile still in place, while the others' sceptical expressions remained intact.

"Involved with the vampires?" Gwyn asked. "What exactly does that mean?"

"I'm not obligated to give specifics." Xavier glanced at his boss as if hoping *he* might offer some enlightenment, but none came. "But it's clear that one of you hasn't been up-front about their history. Who in here has had a reason to draw the ire of the local vampires?"

A prolonged pause ensued, drawn with tension. Then Val sighed. "Right. Fine, I guess I should speak up."

Xavier swivelled to her in surprise. "You?"

"Not me, but the rest of us all know exactly who in this room has a history with the vampires," Val said. "The same person who's still refusing to tell us where she was at the time of Evan's murder."

All eyes turned to Freya.

Her eyes narrowed, passing over each of us like a laser beam as she rose from her seat. "This unfortunate death has nothing to do with my history. Certainly, there's no part of this discussion that needs to be witnessed by a human."

"Except you're doing your best to *avoid* having a discussion," Val retorted. "How about a confession instead? Go on, own up."

"I would talk to you alone, Freya," the Grim Reaper said in his coldest, most resonant tone.

A tense moment passed before the other Reapers rose to their feet and glided from the room. Xavier and I made to do the same, but the Grim Reaper shook his head imperceptibly, and his apprentice stilled, retaking his seat. I did likewise, fighting the urge to draw my arms protectively around my chest. Freya's aura was positively murderous, and she still had yet to retake her seat.

"Tell me the truth," the Grim Reaper said to her. "I will have no patience for lies. What history do you have with the vampires?"

"This is a confidential matter, concerning a task assigned to me by the Reaper Council itself."

"The Council...?" Xavier spoke in a hushed voice. "They

assigned you to work with the vampires? Or were you in charge of Reaping their souls?"

I exhaled sharply in a gasp. Shadows crept around Freya's body, and a sudden shock of bitter coldness numbed all sensation in my fingers and toes.

"I will tell the truth if the human leaves the room." She said this without so much as looking at me.

"The truth is obvious," said the Grim Reaper. "You hunted vampires' souls and fear retribution should they become aware of that history more widely."

The tightening around her mouth told me he'd guessed right. Frankly, I wasn't sure which was more alarming: the fact that she'd hunted the souls of vampires—and there was a department among the Reapers responsible for that—or the fact that she'd lied to the Grim Reaper.

No wonder Evangeline had come to talk to me in person. That Freya had reaped the souls of *vampires* would certainly make her a target for trouble, but it hadn't been her who'd died but an apprentice of one of the other Reapers, someone with no connection to her except in profession.

Strangely, some of my fear lifted at the obvious discomfort in Freya's expression. The shadows around her body had retreated too. She knew she was in the wrong.

"I assume that means you and Evangeline have met?" I risked asking. "The local vampire leader?"

"Obviously," Freya said without looking at me. "Evangeline has been leader of this town's vampires since centuries before your human life began. Now, Charon, I've told you what you need to know. It's time to cease this ridiculous diversion."

"You were reluctant to talk about this for a reason," Xavier said, undeterred. "Also, you haven't mentioned *which* vampires' souls you Reaped. Were any of them members of the group known as the Founders?"

"The details are classified."

Likely, she had, given the sheer number of vampires who'd been involved with the Founders in the centuries in which they'd operated. The vampires were rarely neutral on the subject. Either they were with the Founders or they were against them. And if she'd Reaped any of their souls, that might have been enough to earn a grudge for the rest of her eternal life.

"None of this is remotely relevant to the tragic death of one of our apprentices," she added. "Surely you see that, Charon."

"We shall see," said the Grim Reaper. "I will request more information from the Council. In the meantime, you two can leave."

That was it? Did he not think that the Founders' grudge might extend to the other Reapers, or had he decided to take over the questioning himself? Probably it was for the best if he did, but I still felt wrong-footed as I followed Xavier from the room, rubbing my hands together to restore some sensation in my fingertips.

"What do you think?" I asked Xavier in an undertone. "Do you think she might have drawn the Founders' anger and led them to target the summit?"

"The Founders are definitely ones to hold grudges," he said, "but there's no reason for them to kill an unrelated apprentice. Unless they meant to target Lara instead and didn't know which apprentice was hers."

"I don't know. I feel like Evangeline would have mentioned if the Founders were actually in town." Or would she? You never really knew with the vampires' leader. "Maybe she was just being overly cautious. That's a possibility."

But her warning wasn't something I could easily overlook. For one thing, the Founders were certainly known for targeting innocent people to get their way. While the killer was more likely to be a Reaper than anyone else, the Founders had worked with a Reaper themselves, and their recent endeavours suggested their fellow scythe-wielding immortals had been fresh in their minds.

"I'll walk you home," said Xavier. "You shouldn't worry about us. Evangeline has reason to be on edge, but honestly, there's no need for her *or* the Reapers to keep dragging you into this."

"I tried telling her that. She didn't listen." I put up my umbrella again and beckoned Jet out of the shadow of the tree he'd hidden in to get away from the rain. The little crow swooped ahead while Xavier and I walked out of the cemetery together.

"Do you really think the Founders were involved?" Xavier asked after a moment's pause.

"I have no idea." I exhaled in a sigh. "On the surface, it seems unlikely, but the Founders have definitely tried to recruit from among the Reapers. We know that too."

His expression clouded. "You're right, but Freya is stubborn, and no usual interrogation method will work on a Reaper who doesn't want to divulge their secrets, even magical means of questioning someone to get the truth."

"Yeah, I guess you're as immune to truth potions and spells as you are to vampire mind reading." I racked my thoughts. "What we need is someone else with inside knowledge on the Founders who might be able to confirm her story."

He shook his head. "It's too dangerous to visit Evangeline's prisoners even if they're locked behind bars. You know they'll play mind games with you and won't reveal any actual information."

"I know, but I'll also get another chance to ask Evangeline some questions," I said. "Such as why she didn't just mention

Freya by name if they met. It seems a waste of time forcing me to go through that charade when she knew perfectly well who she wanted to direct my suspicions to."

"It does." We reached the library's doorstep, and he leaned in to kiss me. "I have to get back home tonight, but I'll see you tomorrow?"

"Yeah. I'll see you then." *If the Grim Reaper doesn't say otherwise.*

I entered the library to find a worried-looking Estelle cleaning up what looked like a small mountain of tinsel.

"Sylvester objected to you going out again," she said in explanation. "Honestly, so did Cass. I heard her swearing up a storm upstairs."

"Weird." I hadn't thought Cass would care either way unless she was expressing her displeasure at Evangeline's unexpected visit. "It was fine, really. Better than the last time."

I relayed what I'd learned of Freya's history, which didn't take long since I'd left with more questions than I'd started with. Despite the confirmed link between one of our suspects and the vampires, Aunt Adelaide and Estelle agreed that paying the prisoners a visit was out of the question.

"Spoilsports," said Aunt Candace, who'd naturally taken on the contrary position. "It sounds like they're just the people to help get to the bottom of this. Wouldn't you rather Rory visited them before the Reapers send one of their own people into Evangeline's dungeon?"

From her tone, *she* didn't mind either way, but a Reaper entering the vampires' home would certainly end badly. "That's what I thought. We don't need a Reaper–vampire standoff."

"Then they can finish one another off," Cass said. "Let it go, Rory. Do something else. Like, you know, your job."

"That was uncalled for," Estelle said before I could object.

"Also, Cass, the library has been closed all day, and it's the holidays. She's not doing any less work than you are."

Cass ignored her sister's pointed comment. "Yeah, and I'd like to enjoy Christmas without waiting to wake up with a Reaper's scythe hovering over my bed."

"That would make *my* Christmas," said Aunt Candace with a grin. "Perhaps I shall put in a request. I'm sure one of them will oblige."

"Please don't," I said. "That goes double for the vampires. I really do think they're the ones with the answers more than anyone else."

"And you think the vampires will answer your questions?" Cass glowered at me. "When have they ever been straightforward with you?"

She had me there. "I'll think about it. This isn't something I can sit out of, though. If the Reapers are stuck in town for the duration, we're in for a hell of a gloomy festive season. And I'm not going to leave Xavier to spend the holidays with the other apprentices in that creepy house."

Cass grunted. "What do apprentice Reapers do for fun, anyway? Play chess? Or are they more into solitaire?"

"I have no idea." I figured Laney would already be paying the vampires a visit that evening, but she was the person I *least* wanted to take into that dungeon with me.

I let the subject drop until early evening. When Laney came downstairs, I told her all about the day's events. As expected, she was suitably outraged at how the Reapers had treated me.

"I can't believe they forced you to work as their murder investigator and then treated you like crap," she fumed. "Maybe I should pay them a visit myself. If I can catch the killer in action, so much the better."

"I wouldn't risk it." I continued my account and finished

by telling her about Freya's history with the vampires and my thoughts about speaking to Evangeline's prisoners.

"I can go to the jail and speak to them myself," she said. "See if I can rattle them a bit."

I swallowed, dread creeping up my throat. "You know what happened last time."

"They don't have any more of that poison," she said. "Anyway, Evangeline wants to speak to me, so I'd already planned to go to the vampires' home."

"Please tell me she doesn't have you spying on the Founders again," I said.

"You'd better not," Cass said. "What is with you people trying to get yourselves killed?"

Her tone was unnecessarily harsh, and even Laney raised a brow in surprise. The pair had been mostly civil to one another recently, Cass's weird behaviour at the party aside.

"I was already going to Evangeline's house," said Laney. "What's the problem?"

"Never mind." I hastened to cut in. "Laney, I'll go with you. It's no problem."

Cass threw up her hands and walked away, tossing a caustic "Your funeral" over her shoulder.

"She hasn't had me spying on the Founders, for the record," said Laney. "But I'll try to talk Evangeline into letting us into the dungeon to talk to her unpleasant guests if it puts your mind at ease."

In truth, the mere thought of either of us setting foot in that dungeon made me break out in a cold sweat, but I had to face my fears eventually. If the Founders had a part to play, one of their allies might point me in the right direction.

7

Laney and I walked to the vampires' home as swiftly as was possible given my slower human speed was no match for Laney's vampire pace. While it had stopped raining, my breath fogged the air in white puffs and made her lack of the need to breathe even more obvious.

"I'm starting to see the benefits of being without a pulse," I said through chattering teeth.

"I hope that was a joke." She glided partway up the road and doubled back to let me catch up. "I had a question. What if that apprentice was actually bitten by a vampire? Did you check?"

"I don't think Reapers can be turned." Not that I'd asked, but someone would have spotted bite marks on Evan's neck, surely.

"What would a Reaper-vampire look like, I wonder?" she said. "On second thought, I don't really need that mental image."

"Neither do I." My all-too-human heart began to beat faster as we drew closer to the vampires' home. The mansion, which had been converted from an old church, sat alone, surrounded by a fence. The vampires didn't usually need any protection, including from their own kind, but it added to the general atmosphere.

The door opened before either of us laid a hand on it, an indication that Evangeline already knew we were present.

"Elaine." The vampires' leader offered Laney a smile. "And you brought Aurora with you. How intriguing."

"You knew about Freya?" I asked, figuring that I might as well get some answers from her before I made any attempt to speak to her prisoners. "I found out she used to Reap vampires' souls as part of her job. I assume that's what you were hinting at when you came to the library?"

"You speak as if that were no significant matter, Aurora."

"It is," I acknowledged, "but unless you think a vampire might have gone after the Reapers for revenge on her, I don't see the link with the recent murder. The Grim Reaper doesn't either."

"I merely thought it was a piece of information that ought to be available to everyone present at the Reapers' gathering," she said in deceptively casual tones. "She seemed so reluctant to share it with the others by her own effort."

"Which you wouldn't know if you weren't spying on them," Laney added.

"Of course I did," said Evangeline. "Their minds are hidden to me, and I must resort to other means to ascertain if they are a threat to myself or my kin."

"The Grim Reaper won't think that's an adequate excuse." She didn't need me to tell her that. "What of your prisoners, then? Have any of them been behaving strangely since the Reapers arrived in town?"

"No," she said. "And to my knowledge, none have made any escape attempts. They know the consequences if they were to try."

She didn't need to spell it out for me to guess what level

of punishment she inflicted on any escapees. "Maybe, but if any of the Founders might have come to town to target the Reapers, the prisoners are the only people who might have inside knowledge. Can Laney and I ask them a couple of questions?"

"Now, why would I let you do that?" She studied me through intent eyes, doubtless trying to probe my innermost thoughts. I kept an image of a brick wall in the forefront of my mind, drawing on the practise I'd had at keeping her out and knowing I'd need every ounce of effort to keep out the Founders too.

"You aren't to be deterred, are you?" she said. "I find it a pointless exercise for you to talk to individuals who haven't seen the light of day in weeks, but if you want to put yourself through the ordeal…"

"It's that or find any other Founders who might be roaming around the area," Laney said. "Weren't you going to ask me to search for them?"

Evangeline's smile slipped from her face, causing tension to ripple across my shoulders. While it was undeniably true, Evangeline clearly didn't appreciate her protégé's tone. "No," she said. "As we discussed only a few days ago, no sightings have come to my attention."

"That was before the Reapers showed up in town," I pointed out. "You know they're good at hiding themselves, even from other vampires."

"That does not mean my prisoners have the faintest idea if any are present in town," she said in tones laced with displeasure. "If there was a confession to be extracted, I would have done so myself. But if you must assuage your curiosity, come this way."

She beckoned us into the house. Taking in a deep breath, I followed her. The interior of the vampires' home was as impressive as ever, if intentionally neglected. Cobwebs spanned the stained glass windows and looped between the high pillars supporting the arched ceilings. Similarly to the Reapers' house, the air was colder inside than out, and my breath puffed out in clouds as I walked down the narrow staircase into the dungeon.

There weren't a large number of prisoners in there, but even having four Founders in the same place was too many, in my opinion. Evangeline flat-out refused to have them transferred elsewhere, and since the vampires had managed to break out of the regular jail more than once, I had to admit they were more secure in here than the alternative.

The latest prisoner was a man named Shaw Senior, one of the newest vampires to be turned and the most recent to join the Founders' ranks. His foolish son was imprisoned in the regular jail as he hadn't turned into a vampire. Shaw Junior certainly wouldn't know anything about rogue Founders roaming around, and for all I knew, his father wouldn't either, but he was the person who'd most recently had contact with Mortimer Vale.

Spotting the stocky middle-aged man seated inside the cagelike cell nearest the stairs, I made a beeline for him first.

"Aurora Hawthorn." His eyes glimmered with hate. "You dare to show your face in front of me after what you did?"

"Considering you're the one imprisoned, yes, I think I do dare." Some of my apprehension faded as an unexpected wave of dislike crashed over me. I hadn't forgotten what he'd done to Xavier, and besides, he was far less dangerous than the five Reapers whose company I'd spent entirely too much of my day in. "I have some questions for you."

"What?" he growled. "What do you want with me?"

"Mortimer Vale," I said. "When did you last see him? Did he tell you if he had—" I'd been trying to hold back from showing my hand too early, but I didn't know how else to get to the point without being drawn into vampire mind games. "Did he tell you anything?" I finished vaguely.

"Did he?" He laughed shortly. "No, he didn't tell me the Founders' plans if that's what you mean. Wouldn't tell me a damn thing. Will you leave me alone now?"

"He's your sire," said Laney. "Surely he gave you access to *some* inside information."

"He's your sire too." His mouth curved into a cruel smile. "I bet that bothers you. Both of you, in fact."

Oh, boy. I'd been so wrapped up in all the other things that might possibly go wrong with this interrogation that I'd momentarily forgotten Laney and Shaw had both been bitten by the same vampire. *Not a welcome reminder.*

"So?" Laney raised a brow. "He doesn't tell *me* his plans, but that's because I hate his guts. You don't."

"Did Mortimer Vale order you to make those potions?" I returned to the pertinent matter at hand. "Was it all him? Did you give them to anyone else?"

A humourless laugh escaped him. "You think that because I'm behind bars, you have the right to ask me irrelevant questions?"

"Actually, I think we have the right to do worse than that." Laney leaned closer to his cell. Alarmed, I reached for her shoulder, but she withdrew a second later, shaking her head.

"He doesn't know if anyone else has them."

"You dare to infiltrate my thoughts?" He leaned against the cage bars and bared his sharp teeth right back at her. "You will pay for this when I get out of here."

"But you won't." Laney shook her head pityingly. "You're the least threatening vampire I've ever met."

"You read his mind," I whispered as we walked away. "Anything there?"

"Nothing," she muttered. "Let's try the next one."

My heart began to beat faster as we reached the next

occupied cell. Victoire lounged on a bench, a smile on her pristine face. How she managed to look as if she had access to a hair salon and full makeup while behind bars, I'd probably never know.

As we approached her cell, I made my mind as blank as I could manage. She might carry a vampire's typical intimidating air, but she wasn't the most manipulative of the prisoners in Evangeline's home. That honour went to Carlos Verdant, and I was saving him for last. Victoire had been his apprentice at one time but had allied with Mortimer Vale more recently, going against her own sire and former master. That was the small part of vampires' convoluted histories that I knew; the rest went far beyond my understanding, but unlike Shaw, she'd been a vampire a very long time—long enough, perhaps, to have known Freya in her former life.

"Well?" she said invitingly. "To what do I owe the pleasure?"

"I have something I want to talk to you about," I said. "The Grim Reaper."

Her smile gained an amused edge. "What of him?"

"You have a history," I said. "I want to know what it is."

Her head tilted on one side. "Why not ask him yourself?"

"You know he doesn't share his secrets with mortals," I said, undeterred. "Besides, I thought you were determined to convince me the Reapers were the bad guys."

She uttered a delicate laugh, one without any humour in it. "And I was under the impression you refused to be swayed from your trust in Charon."

"I wouldn't say I *trust* him, but I sure don't trust you either." I knew she was trying to probe the barrier around my thoughts, and I opted for just enough honesty to seem plausible without giving away anything of note. "How were you two involved?"

"Involved. Such a dull word." She shook her head. "He

amuses me. All the Reapers do, with their commitment to rule-following and their insistence upon control over a very uncontrollable process. It so irks them when one of my kind disrupts that process."

"By turning someone into a vampire, I know," Laney said. "Anyway, Evangeline has known him just as long, and I don't think she's ever called him a friend or acquaintance or whatever you claim to be. Anyway, since we're on the subject, do you know any other Reapers, especially any who joined your little cult?"

"Why exactly would I tell you that?" she enquired.

"Because you're stuck in here and don't have anywhere else to go," said Laney. "And Rory and I aren't going anywhere until you answer."

I flashed her a warning look. I drew the line at standing in the vampires' dungeon all night, waiting for Victoire to let something useful slip, but neither did I want to leave Laney in here alone without backup. No way.

"Yes, Aurora seems to be awfully quiet." She smiled at me. "Are you the one who's been fretting about my past dalliances with Charon?"

"Why didn't you use his name when you were visiting?" Not the most relevant question, but I couldn't believe I'd lived here a year and had always assumed everyone called him *Grim Reaper.*

Her laugh echoed around the cell. "I preferred his old name, truth be told, but the Reapers do like to commemorate the moment they cast off their mortal lives."

"Old name?" The obvious dawned. "You knew him back when he was human."

"Oh." Laney gaped at her too. "You two had *that* kind of history. No wonder he doesn't like you much now. You remind him of what he's missing out on."

"I think that's quite enough for now." A warning note

entered her voice though her smile remained in place. I should have taken that as a sign, but her revelation had kicked off another cascade of questions in my mind, and it took a moment for me to remember that Charon wasn't the Reaper I'd originally intended to ask her about.

"What of the other Reapers?" I asked. "Have you had any history with them? Especially the ones tasked with Reaping vampires' souls?"

It wasn't the smoothest way to bring up the subject, but we'd drifted far from our original purpose, and my words certainly had an effect. All hint of mirth vanished from her expression. "I'd be careful, Aurora. My kind are not forgiving of those who threaten our immortal lives."

Enough to murder someone over it? "I just wondered if you'd met any recently."

She rose from the bench. "If Charon is considering a change in profession, I would strongly advise him against it."

"He… What?" Was that even an option? "No. He isn't. Never mind. I was more wondering if the Founders were generally aware of which Reapers to avoid." The phrase sounded ridiculous even as it was leaving my mouth. The Founders had no power whatsoever over *any* Reapers. Wasn't that why they'd started developing those potions in the first place, to target one of their immortal enemies' few weaknesses?

"Surely you run tests on people you recruit," said Laney. "I mean, if you're actively recruiting Reapers as allies, you wouldn't want to accidentally hire someone who used their scythe on one of your friends."

"We are *not* recruiting Reapers."

"Your friend Carlos Verdant did," I reminded her.

"Now, you saw for yourself that dear Carlos and I are no longer allied."

"No, you switched sides to Mortimer Vale instead," I said. "Did *he* employ any Reapers?"

Granted, I'd seen no evidence that Vale had any Reaper allies during our prior encounters. She'd also given no hint that she knew about the Reapers' ongoing summit. Even if she and Freya had once crossed paths at any point in the past, there were no obvious connections between the pair of them.

"You're wasting your time, Aurora," she said. "Aside from dear Charon, my interactions with Reapers have been minimal. I generally find them tedious."

Given that she'd already double-crossed Carlos Verdant by the time he'd brought in his rogue Reaper ally, she might well be telling the truth. She'd also been incarcerated by the time Shaw Senior had employed the anti-Reaper potion against Xavier, and I had no reason to believe she held any extra knowledge on the subject.

That left one person in this dungeon who might know of any recent activity involving the Founders and the Reapers: Carlos Verdant, my least favourite of an already unappealing group.

The sophisticated vampire sat in a cell at the very end of the row. Like Victoire, he was not in the least diminished by his imprisonment, his hair glossy and his pale face positively glowing.

"Aurora." He pronounced my name as though one might refer to a fatal disease. "I wouldn't waste your time with me. I have no idea what my fellow Founders are planning due to my unjust incarceration in this cell."

"Unjust?" said Laney. "You tried to murder us. Now, we want to know the truth. Which other Reapers did you work with aside from the one at your creepy lab?"

Irritation flickered across his face. "If it's the Reapers you want information on, why not ask them yourself?"

Did that mean he knew the summit was in town? I hastily blanked my mind in case he'd picked up on that thought, but the cruel smile tugging at his mouth told me I'd been too late.

"It strikes me as a dangerous time to invite Reapers to Ivory Beach," he said, "but I expect Charon is trying to prove the situation is under control. He and Evangeline have that much in common."

"You know his name too." *You don't say, Rory.*

"Our history is as entwined as any who have lived as long as we," he said dismissively. "You should focus on your petty human concerns while you can."

"And what's that supposed to mean?" Laney bared her teeth at him. "Was that a threat?"

It wasn't one I hadn't heard before, and nothing in his choice of words indicated he knew anything had gone awry at the Reapers' summit any more than the others did.

"Your history is entwined because they Reap your souls too." I expected retaliation and was surprised when he remained seated, his face expressionless. "When one of you dies, a Reaper shows up. Do you—"

"The Reapers' influence is fading," he said. "They will soon be no threat to us at all."

"You—" I jerked back sharply when he was suddenly on his feet, his unblemished white teeth rasping against the cage bars.

"I think that's quite enough." Evangeline spoke from the stairs near the dungeon's entrance. "I shall finish this myself, Aurora, Elaine."

Laney didn't budge, but I found myself backing away instinctively. Despite my rational mind knowing that a cage lay between me and the angry vampire, those bars suddenly looked awfully flimsy.

"Come." Evangeline beckoned with a crooked finger, and with visible reluctance, Laney withdrew too.

When we reached the top of the stairs, Evangeline turned on us, her eyes dark in the dimly lit space. "Is your curiosity satisfied?"

"No, and Carlos Verdant all but admitted he's plotting to bring down the Reapers," I said heatedly. "What if he—"

"He's made the same claim at least once a week since his imprisonment began," she said. "If he spoke true, Charon would be naught but a pile of dust, but the last I checked, he was as living as a Reaper can be."

"Still." I pressed a hand to my thumping heart. "You might want to press him on his knowledge about those potions. We never got to that part."

"No," she said. "It seems a waste of time, in my view. My prisoners know nothing of note."

"Except the Grim Reaper's name," I said. "You do too."

Evangeline and the Grim Reaper were connected by more than their mutual longevity, but I found myself hoping fervently that she hadn't been involved with him in the same manner as Victoire had. I had enough nightmare fuel in my brain already.

"A name means little on its own," was her enigmatic answer. "Is this remotely relevant to this murder you're supposedly fixated on solving?"

Well... no. "Not exactly, but if you have all this tangled history, it makes it even more likely that someone with a grudge against one of the Reapers in that house went after their apprentice. How widely known among the Founders are the Reapers who take away the souls of dead vampires?"

Tension rippled in the air as her eyes raked over me. "I would tread carefully with your questioning."

"I'm only asking if you and the other vampires knew the identity of which Reapers were given the task of reaping your souls."

"We might have known if we were acquainted with those

who perished at their hands," she said. "Otherwise, we were no more aware than the public at large."

I'd have to take her word for it on that, and admittedly, it was very unlikely that a vampire who died would be able to identify the Reaper who took their soul, nor that they would be able to tell tales to the others on who was behind the hooded cloak. While several vampires had died during our time in this town, I hadn't seen who'd taken their souls, and even Xavier hadn't known the details of the process.

"Do you think there is a chance we have another rogue in the area?" I asked. "Or is it more likely that someone in the house was behind the murder?"

"I believe the latter," said Evangeline. "Now, I will ask you to leave, Aurora. I have vampires to instruct."

"Including me," Laney said. "You want me to hunt for the Founders?"

"I want you to keep your eyes open," she corrected. "And do nothing rash, either on your own account or on behalf of your friend."

The meaning was clear, but my curiosity was slow to die, pun intended.

Vampires and Reapers. Their immortal lives had been tangled for centuries, and I was caught in the middle, just like my dad had been.

8

When Laney and I exited the vampires' home, it took me a moment to spot the other person lurking outside in the shadows near the door.

"Cass?" Laney frowned at her. "What are you doing?"

"Nothing." My cousin shuffled into view, looking as close to sheepish as I'd ever seen her. Had she followed us all the way here from the library?

"Something you wanted from Evangeline?" I queried.

"Definitely not," she muttered under her breath. "Let's go home."

What's with her? Had she thought we might run into trouble while questioning the Founders? Laney studied her face in puzzlement, but Cass was impossible even for a vampire to read, not least thanks to the pendant she wore that prevented anyone from scanning her mind.

"All right," Laney said. "I'll head to my meeting with Evangeline. You two can walk back to the library together."

Cass looked about as thrilled as if she'd been asked to clean up after Sylvester had vomited tinsel everywhere, which seemed a bit unfair. She and I had never been best friends, but we'd turned a corner in the past few months, and she was usually civil toward me, if not outright friendly.

"What did you think would happen?" I asked her. "That the Founders would escape? Or something like—like what happened to Laney last time?"

"Stop talking."

"You just want to walk home in silence?" I buried my hands in my pockets, shivering in the chill air. "All right."

If it was Laney she wanted to speak to, she might have waited until after Evangeline was done with her. I knew that Aunt Adelaide, for one, would disapprove of her daughter hanging around the vampires' house all night, and Cass was usually too cautious to take an unnecessary risk like that. I was surprised she'd come this far.

I glanced at her again. "You could have told Laney you came for moral support. She wouldn't have minded."

"I told you to be quiet." She strode ahead down the darkened high street, past the cemetery gates. There, I slowed, peering over the fence, wondering if the Reapers had gotten any further with the questioning since I'd left and if the Council had supplied the information on Freya's history that the Grim Reaper had requested.

"What are you looking at?" Cass backtracked to my side and reached to pull me away from the fence. "Don't you even think about going back in there."

"I wasn't." I began walking again. "I was just—"

A sudden loud growl drowned out my words, then something large and shaggy came barrelling through the darkness. The creature resembled a cross between a dog and a lion, albeit formed of what appeared to be shadows. As I backed away, the shadowy being passed *through* the fence and leapt straight at Cass and me.

"Hey!" Cass whipped out her wand and cast a spell,

conjuring a stream of rippling light that shot straight at the monster.

The beam of light from her wand passed straight through the beast as if it wasn't there. *Whoa.* It was as if the beast was only half present, but its sharp teeth appeared solid enough to bite. Heart racing, I grabbed my own wand and backed farther downhill. If we kept going, it'd follow us back to the library, and for all I knew, it'd be able to jump straight through the front door of our home without any resistance.

My spell went straight through our attacker too, fizzling out on contact with the ground. "Dammit. I have to call Xavier."

Problem: He was somewhere on the other side of that monster.

"Watch out!" yelled a voice.

A second later, Reid came running out from amid the headstones. When he lifted a hand, the beast turned toward him, darkness swirling around its large paws.

Then a window appeared in midair, right behind the monster. Its large shadowy feet slipped on the edge, its paws flailed, and as Reid caught up to us, the beast vanished through the window into the dark.

"Rory!" Xavier ran up as the doorway blinked out of existence, staring at the spot where the beast had vanished. "What was that?"

"I don't know." Shivers raced over my skin. "A monster. Whatever it was, our spells had no effect on it."

"And Reid banished it?"

Reid gulped. "I think so. I've never done that before."

"Good job, since it might have attacked anyone else in the street," said Xavier. "Where did it come from? Who summoned it?"

"You should be asking your fellow Reapers those questions, not us," said Cass. "Since one of them tried to kill us."

"Why?" He looked between me and Cass. "Why were you two walking down here at night?"

"We went to see… the vampires." I wasn't sure if I wanted Reid to know that, but he had just saved my life, and Cass looked to be on the brink of walking off without even saying thank you. "Was that monster sent after us on purpose, or did we just happen to get in the way?"

"It wasn't corporeal?" Xavier turned toward Reid, who hesitantly shook his head. "I'm not sure you *were* the targets. There are a lot more dangerous creatures in the afterworld that would prove deadly to a human. That one… What was it, a hellbeast?"

Reid shuddered. "I don't know."

"Aren't you the one who banished it?" Cass said, none too kindly. "Both of you need to find whoever in that house of yours summoned that thing before they do it again."

Xavier's expression darkened. "Yes, we need to report this immediately."

The Grim Reaper would not be happy to know someone had summoned a monster on his property, and doubtless everyone would be subjected to another round of questioning. As little as I wanted to leave Xavier to face them alone, I'd spent entirely too much of my day in that house and had received zero gratitude from his boss. Staying all night wouldn't do me any favours.

"Do that," said Cass. "And if one of your monsters shows up at the library, I'll set my manticore on it and on the rest of you for good measure."

"You have a manticore?" Reid blanched.

"Oh, I have worse." Cass bared her teeth, vampire-style. "I'm not scared of the dead. As you saw yourself, Reaper."

"Cass," I muttered. "Simmer down."

"You two should go back to the library," Xavier said. "I'll come and talk to you tomorrow, okay?"

"Sure thing." I didn't blame him for not offering to walk back with me, given Cass's mood. She stalked ahead of me, fury etched on her face, and forced me to jog to catch up with her.

"Really, he did save our lives," I puffed out. "Reid did. You might've thanked him for it."

"I don't like him," she shot over her shoulder. "If all the Reapers' apprentices are that clueless, it's no wonder one of them got murdered."

She entered the library first, where we found a concerned Aunt Adelaide pacing the area in front of the door.

"Oh, there you are, Rory." She surveyed Cass with surprise. "I didn't know Cass went out with you and Laney."

Cass flashed me a warning look that prompted me to avoid the subject and start off with the more important part of the update. "We were attacked by some kind of monster on the way back."

We went into the living room to explain. Estelle and Aunt Candace joined us too, pursued by the latter's floating pen and notepad, and listened in shock to our account of the attack.

"One of the Reapers set a monster on you?" said Aunt Candace. "Jealous, were they?"

"Candace, this is serious," said Aunt Adelaide. "*Was* it one of the Reapers?"

"Who else knows the afterworld and its monsters?" I said. "The beast came out of the cemetery, which suggests it was summoned somewhere on the Reaper's property, but I have no idea which of them did it."

"What kind of monster was it?" asked Estelle.

"Some kind of hellbeast, according to Xavier," Cass supplied. "Whatever *that* means."

"He said it wasn't corporeal," I added. "It jumped *through* the fence, and none of our spells left a scratch on it."

"Like a ghost but a thousand times uglier," Cass said.

"Xavier said it wasn't the most dangerous thing that might have come out of the afterworld," I said. "It's not the sort of beast that preys on humans, but it's still dangerous."

"The library's security ought to keep out anything hostile, ghosts included," said Aunt Adelaide. "What worries me is that they haven't caught the summoner yet."

"Of course they have," Cass said impatiently. "All the suspects are still in that house. And if you hadn't decided to question the vampires, you wouldn't have made yourself into a target."

"The vampires had nothing to do with this." Or had they? Perhaps they had, if one of them had indeed been the summoner, but I had a hard time believing that. "Also, Laney was already on her way to see Evangeline, whether I'd decided to go with her or not."

Cass gave a soft snort and walked out of the living room without offering a reply.

Estelle watched her leave, her brow furrowed in confusion. "Did Cass follow you to the vampires' house?"

"I think it was Laney she followed," I explained, "to make sure the Founders didn't hurt her again."

"Did you learn anything from the vampires?" asked Aunt Adelaide.

"Not about the murder," I said. "The prisoners don't know a great deal about what's going on outside. They do know the Grim Reaper's real name, but apparently, that's common knowledge among the vampires anyway."

"It is?" said Estelle. "I guess they've all been around for centuries, long enough to know each other pretty well, even if they aren't friends."

"Well… I actually think the Grim Reaper and Victoire had an affair."

"What?" said both Aunt Adelaide and Estelle at the same

moment, while Aunt Candace let out a shriek then broke into hysterical laughter while her pen scribbled so rapidly on her notepad that ink sprayed all over the carpet.

"Candace!" Aunt Adelaide ran to clean it up, while Aunt Candace continued to guffaw.

"It's not *that* funny," I said to her. "It's kinda creepy, actually."

"Definitely," said Estelle. "I don't think I want to think about the Grim Reaper being romantically involved with anyone. Even if he was human at the time."

"That's equally weird," I added. "Anyway, that's all I learned from Evangeline's prisoners. Victoire has no contact with the outside world. Carlos Verdant too. He worked out that we have Reapers visiting but not that one of them is dead. Also, Laney read Shaw's mind and confirmed Mortimer Vale didn't tell him a thing, and he's the person most likely to have had recent contact with the Founders."

"What was with Evangeline's warning, then?" asked Estelle. "Do the prisoners know one of the Reapers used to be tasked with taking vampires' souls?"

"I'm not sure they do." I thought back to Victoire's anger and Carlos Verdant's ominous statement. "I believe Evangeline when she says they haven't escaped in the past few weeks. If there's a vampire involved in this murder, it's an outsider who isn't in communication with them."

"I don't know that anything we spoke to the vampires about was that significant." I rubbed my forehead. "Also, I don't know of any vampires who make a habit of summoning things from the afterworld. I'm not sure they even can."

"Maybe you need to speak to more vampires," Aunt Candace said. "In fact, I can—"

"No," her sister interrupted. "We've had quite enough of our family members being placed in danger for one day."

I had to agree despite my lingering questions. Had one of the Reapers been responsible for setting that beast on us, or had someone else been trying to frame them? Who else would have had the knowledge or inclination? Even the library contained no books with information on afterworld monsters. The Reapers kept that knowledge to themselves, and even my dad's history with them hadn't made him privy to that information as far as I knew.

And if it *was* one of the Reapers—such as Freya, trying to cover her tracks—why set a monster on us that didn't appear to be able to inflict any physical damage? Perhaps I'd misread what Xavier had implied by *incorporeal.* Ghosts couldn't do much except throw things around, which had admittedly been hazardous when paired with a setting like the library, but otherwise, they couldn't leave a mark on any living creature.

If any information whatsoever existed in the library, it lay between the covers of the aptly titled Book of Questions. With that in mind, I found the black-covered tome in its usual place behind the front desk, but I'd scarcely picked it up before the owl landed on the desk inches from my head. Sylvester spread his vast tawny wings, knocking the Book of Questions out of my hand.

"Don't bother," he said as I scrambled to pick it up.

"I'm not going to ask about the murder," I said to him. "An afterworld monster just attacked us. I want to know what it was."

"It sounds like one of your Reaper friends already banished the monster, you overly inquisitive pencil," he said. "Have you ever thought that your penchant for asking too many questions is the reason things keep trying to eat you?"

"The monster didn't try to eat us." But he might have had a point there. "Fine, I'll go ask the guardian instead."

I'd spoken without thinking—a bad idea, as it turned out.

In an instant, a sudden shower of tinsel came tumbling onto my head. The owl took flight with a hoot of laughter as I flailed around and tried to free myself.

"Sylvester!"

Great one, Rory. The Book of Questions and the fourth-floor corridor's guardian were not friends, though they shared the mutual goal of protecting the library from harm, and I should have known better than to invoke its name in front of Sylvester.

"Rory, what did you do?" Estelle's voice was muffled through layers of tinsel.

I pushed a handful of silver sparkles out of my eyes and sighed. "I was going to ask the Book of Questions to identify that monster. When Sylvester refused, I suggested asking the guardian upstairs, and… you saw how well he took that."

"Ah." She helped me pull more tinsel out of my hair. "I'm not sure that the guardian would be able to help either. I can't think of any wishes that would apply to this situation, since the library can only affect what's inside its walls, not outside."

She was right. I couldn't simply wish for the enemy to be found and brought to justice. The world didn't work like that, and besides, the guardian's knowledge was confined to what my grandmother had given it and no more—certainly nothing related to the afterworld.

As for the vampires, our meeting had been a dead end—pun intended—but where did that leave the investigation into Evan's murder? And if we hadn't been the targets for whoever had summoned that monster, who had?

9

My dreams that night consisted of a montage of giant monsters, occasionally covered in tinsel, and I woke itching all over despite having cleaned off the aftermath of Sylvester's attack the previous night. A closer inspection showed me that my hair had acquired a new coating of silver sparkles at some point in the early hours, suggesting Sylvester had not yet forgiven me for my comment about the guardian.

That owl. Cursing him under my breath, I showered thoroughly to wash every trace of tinsel from me. Then I groaned when I left my room and found a new trail of silver leading down the landing.

"It's a nightmare, isn't it?" Estelle stuck her head out of her room. "Honestly, I'm thinking of buying tinsel next year that disintegrates a day after Christmas."

"Is that a thing?" I trod carefully around the trail of glittering tinsel to avoid any sticking to my feet.

"Not that I know of, but someone must have thought of the idea." Yawning, she came out of her room. "Did you sleep all right?"

"Not really," I admitted. "Too much on my mind."

I'd stayed awake until I heard the soft tread of Laney's quiet feet outside the door, at which point I'd passed out cold. I'd known rationally that she wouldn't be in any real danger if that monster came back, but there was still the chance Evangeline had sent her out to hunt for rogue vampires again or else spy on the Reapers. Frankly, I wasn't sure which was worse.

"At least we won't have many visitors today," said Estelle. "It'll be quiet here until New Year's Eve, I bet."

Unless the entire Reaper Council descends on the town. Hadn't the Grim Reaper been planning to contact them to confirm Freya's claims? Or had that intention been forgotten when Xavier had to tell him that Cass and I had been attacked right outside his home? I didn't know, but while we'd been spared an overnight visit from our scythe-wielding adversary, I had the sneaking suspicion that he wouldn't let the previous night's incidents go unnoticed.

Estelle and I were finishing breakfast when the inevitable knock came on the front door. I downed the rest of my coffee and went to answer. While Xavier stood alone on the doorstep, my usual happiness at seeing him was tinged with wariness.

"Are you all right?" he asked, kissing me gently on the lips.

"I'm fine." I steeled myself. "Did the Grim Reaper send you?"

"Sorry." Contrition flitted across his face. "He wants to hear your account of the attack last night. I convinced him to wait until morning, but he's insistent."

"There's nothing I can give him that Reid didn't already tell him, is there?"

"He still wants to hear from you," he said apologetically. "Or your cousin."

"Cass? She'd sooner jump off the pier than play nice with the Reapers." I suppressed a sigh. "All right."

It was another cold, drizzly day, and I huddled inside my coat as Xavier and I walked across the square toward the high street.

"I'm impressed you managed to keep him distracted all night," I remarked. "What did he do, interrogate Reid and then go back to questioning the Reapers about Evan's death? Did he have time to dig into Freya's history?"

"First, he sent us to search the house for any signs of summonings," he replied. "Reapers don't need props to summon beasts from the afterworld, though, so there wasn't anything to be found."

"It was almost certainly a Reaper who called that monster, right?"

He inclined his head. "The trouble is there's no way to communicate with a beast like that even if we summoned it back. It's not like a demon. It can't speak."

A shiver sprang to my arms. "I think I'm glad of that, to be honest. That monster was scary enough on its own."

"Scary or not, it wasn't overtly dangerous to you," he said. "Or to any human. Hellbeasts consume spirits, not living beings."

"They eat… what, ghosts?" Wait. Hadn't we encountered one of those a couple of months ago, summoned for the purposes of devouring a ghost and preventing him from giving away who'd killed him? "Why send it after Cass and me, then?"

"I don't know, but I didn't get a close enough look at the monster to confirm if that's actually what it was," he said. "Your description sounds a lot like a hellbeast, but the others spent a full three hours debating the subject last night."

"Why not ask Reid? I mean, he's the one who banished it."

"Reid got a thorough grilling yesterday, but my boss insisted he wants testimony from you or your cousin as well, just in case there were any details Reid missed."

Maybe he didn't trust the apprentice, which, since everyone in the house was a potential murder suspect, was kind of understandable.

When we reached the cemetery gates, I slowed. "We don't have to talk to the others again, do we?"

"My boss said he wanted to speak to you alone, so I wouldn't think so."

I hope not. Doubtless, they'd been irked at the new development, and it wouldn't surprise me if certain among their group had been disappointed the monster hadn't been the sort that killed the living instead of the dead.

Xavier and I found the Grim Reaper alone in the meeting room, seated at the long table and waiting expectantly for me.

As soon as I sat down, he spoke. "You will describe the attack, Aurora."

Friendly as ever. I recounted the incident of the previous night the best I could remember it. Then he asked me to explain it again. And again.

"I've told you everything already," I said. "Asking me the same questions isn't going to make it any easier to track down that beast. Doesn't it only eat the dead, not the living?"

Evan. My suspicions grew when the Grim Reaper fixed me with a flat stare that gave the impression that the shadows themselves were staring directly at me.

"Unless," I said slowly, "that was the whole point."

"Yes," Xavier put in. "If it was summoned earlier, when Evan died..."

"It would have stopped his ghost from coming back," I concluded. "Is that the reason you didn't sense his death?"

Chills raced all over my body as the room went even colder than usual until ice coated the insides of the windows. Shadows coiled around the Grim Reaper's hooded form, and my teeth chattered so loudly I almost missed his reply. "Yes. I suspect so."

"The killer tricked you."

And the Grim Reaper's fury knew no bounds. The question was, if the beast had been summoned for the purposes of preventing Evan from returning as a ghost, how had it spent the rest of the day roaming around the property without anyone noticing?

"Only an incredibly skilled Reaper would have been able to get the timing right," Xavier murmured. "The beast would need to have been summoned a moment before Evan's death and set upon him an instant later, devouring Evan's soul before any of us sensed his departure from this world."

"And the monster stuck around afterwards?" I buried my hands in my lap in an attempt to get some sensation back into my fingers. "Can you stop turning this place into a freezer? It's really distracting."

The Grim Reaper ignored both of my comments. "Now," he said, "you understand the need for me to be thorough with my questions."

"There's still nothing more I can tell you," I said. "*Has* the beast been roaming around the house the whole time?"

"That has yet to be determined, but I highly doubt that to be the case," said the Grim Reaper. "One of us would certainly have noticed its presence."

Unless it was hiding in the afterworld. But the afterworld was as easy to sense for a Reaper as the real world, if not more. While the Reapers had spent most of the past day stuck in the meeting room, arguing with one another, surely one of the apprentices would have noticed a monster roaming around the property.

"And there's no way to prove it was summoned inside the house and not elsewhere?"

"No," Xavier said. "Reapers have no need to set up a circle of sage like a human would if they called on anything from the afterworld. Some would still take precautions if summoning a particularly dangerous creature, but that beast wasn't too big of a threat."

"It's still not allowed, right?" I wasn't sure on the legalities of summoning a beast from the afterworld when it was a Reaper who did it and not a regular person, but I had an inkling that "summoning a monster in the Grim Reaper's house" was the kind of thing that got you struck from their Christmas card list.

"Not without the permission of the Council," said the Grim Reaper. "Some would disobey that rule, at their own peril."

Translation: Not every Reaper was as glued to tradition as he was. But from what I'd seen, most of the Reapers present in this house certainly were, which made it hard to imagine any of them summoning a monster on the property.

"What about Freya?" I asked. "Is she still your main suspect? Also, did the Reaper Council confirm she used to Reap vampires' souls?"

"I have yet to make contact with the Council," said the Grim Reaper. "They would want to know of Evan's death. If I were to contact them and not tell them about his murder, I would be breaking the law."

"And not contacting them at all doesn't count as deceiving them?" Reaper logic, apparently. "I thought you needed their confirmation of Freya's history so you could figure out if a vampire was behind this."

"I can manage without it," he said simply. "Nobody else must know of this death, especially the Council."

"Evangeline already does," I said. "She's been spying on you, as she usually does."

Xavier glanced at me as if concerned his boss might react with anger, but the Grim Reaper merely said, "Evangeline is not human. She will not interfere in our business."

Did he really not mind her spying on him? Or did he plan to confront her after the other Reapers had departed? It was little surprise that most of his wrath was reserved for the killer, but the other Reapers surely wouldn't like the idea of a vampire eavesdropping on their top-secret meetings either.

"There's a difference between interfering and helping," I said. "Also, Evan *was* human at one time. Doesn't he have a family who deserve to know how he died and who was responsible?"

"No," he said. "The Reapers are his family."

The firm edge to his tone indicated that he wanted to finish that sentence with, *and that's how it should be*, as if I needed another reminder that Xavier belonged to him alone and not to anyone else, even me.

"What now, then?" I asked. "If you refuse to speak to the Council and gather more evidence, and Freya hasn't confessed to anything yet, you're at a stalemate."

"I don't know that Freya *did* kill him," said Xavier. "She was adamant yesterday that she was innocent, and she doesn't have any motive to attack someone else's apprentice, whatever her history with the vampires."

"Then was it a vampire out for revenge?" I asked of the Grim Reaper. "Can a vampire have done what you suspect and summoned a hellbeast for the purposes of removing evidence of murder?"

"Absolutely not." His tones plunged into icy depths once again. "None could save for one of our own. So, your visit to the vampires yesterday was a pointless risk to your own life."

"Evangeline had already figured out what happened. You

know that," I said. "She gave me a clear warning, and I was justified in wondering if the Founders might be involved after what we learned about Freya's history."

"Speaking to them was not your task to undertake," he said.

"What, were you going to pay them a visit yourself?" I retorted. "You can't force me to take part in your investigation and not let me do anything on my own, especially if the killer *is* the one who sent that monster after us."

"She's right," Xavier said. "Harmless or not, the monster seemed to have been sent to intimidate and scare Rory away from the investigation. That's not something we want to encourage, or else we'd be playing into the killer's hands."

"You overstep, my apprentice. Your vision is clouded by your attachment to that human."

"And yours is equally clouded by your insistence on doing everything by the book," Xavier retorted. "If we'd spoken to the vampires ourselves, like I suggested—"

"You did?" The question slipped out before I could think better of it. "You think this is their work? All we got from them last night is that Carlos Verdant is absolutely convinced that the Reapers aren't going to be a threat to the Founders for much longer, but he didn't give specifics."

"Empty words." The Grim Reaper's tone was as cold as the ice on the inside of the windows. "He knows he faces an infinite number of days behind bars, and he deserves worse."

"You and Evangeline agree on that, actually," I said. "You're still at a stalemate unless you find more proof. Have you thought about examining Evan's body again? The hellbeast might have devoured his soul, but he was already dead by then."

"There isn't a mark on him," said the Grim Reaper. "That line of questioning is pointless. No, we shall tease out the truth through asking the other Reapers of their knowledge concerning that beast, and as you insist upon involving your-self in this, I will ask you to be present."

"You want me to ask them face-to-face if they set a monster on me." He had to be joking. "Didn't you already do that last night? You had plenty of time."

"Since you insist upon conducting questionings with the vampires behind my back," he said, "I would like to ensure that you remain within my sight for the time being."

"I'm supposed to be at work." Nope, he wasn't joking. He really was that paranoid. "You know, at the job you hauled me away from to help you out without showing a jot of gratitude."

"You want my gratitude?"

"I want answers," I corrected. "And some basic respect. I think I've earned that from you after all the crap you've made me put up with recently."

If I'd been braver, I might have alluded to his supposed affair with Victoire in order to take him off guard, but I didn't quite have the nerve. Besides, for all I knew, the subject wouldn't rattle him at all. *Bloody Reapers.*

While he went to fetch the others, Xavier took my hand under the table and squeezed it in reassurance. "He knows we're right. That beast couldn't have been summoned by a non-Reaper. Either someone who was in the house did it or they know who did."

"I hope they're more cooperative than yesterday, then."

Like the previous day, the Reapers entered the room one at a time, starting with Janus. The stoic Reaper's expression remained unchanged throughout our questions.

"I was here in this very room at the time of the attack," he said, "as you yourself can attest, Charon."

"The monster was summoned earlier than that," said Xavier. "Did you see any signs of it in the house? Or in the afterworld?"

"I did not."

"And what of your apprentice?" asked Xavier. "He's the one who banished the monster. Why did he have to deal with it alone?"

"The other Reapers and I were involved in a confidential discussion at the time, as you both know perfectly well." His tone gained an irritated edge as he swivelled toward the Grim Reaper. "I do not permit my apprentice to step out of bounds, unlike some."

The Grim Reaper stared him out, and I found myself fervently glad not to be on the receiving end of his unseen glare. "That concludes the questioning."

When he left, I leaned to Xavier and whispered, "Does that mean you and the other Reaper apprentices were all in the living room at the time the monster was summoned?"

"No, we went our separate ways," he replied. "Lara and Alise had a huge argument yesterday evening, and Reid and I both left the house until they calmed down."

Next to be questioned was Val, who wore her usual assured smile throughout the questions. She also expressed suitable outrage at the monster's attack on Cass and me.

"What a cowardly move," she said. "It's lucky the killer wasn't smart enough to summon something that could cause you any genuine harm."

"It wasn't exactly harmless," I said. "Not to the dead, anyway."

"You don't have too many ghosts in this town, I've noticed," she said. "Charon keeps them away, I expect."

No sense of guilt was evident in her words, and she didn't seem to have concluded that the beast might have been used to remove proof of the cause of Evan's death either. Neither had Janus, come to that.

Gwyn was next. His expression was as stoic as Janus's, and I eyed his giant wolfhound with renewed apprehension, noting the similarities with the beast that had attacked Cass and me. "Hunt… he isn't a real dog, is he? I mean, he's from the afterworld, right?"

"The beast is as real as I am," Gwyn said. "Is this relevant?"

"It might be." I looked at Xavier, whose eyes widened a little. "I mean, so was that monster. Did you summon him—Hunt?"

A shiver trailed down my back as Gwyn's cold eyes locked with mine. "I did, many years ago. As the beast was loyal, I chose to keep him at my side."

"Against my advice," said the Grim Reaper. "Where were you during the attack yesterday?"

While Gwyn stubbornly denied any involvement, I couldn't stop my attention from lingering on the elephant—or wolfhound—in the room. The similarities might have been surface level, but if Gwyn had broken the rules once, might he have done so again? The question of *why* remained a mystery, and when the Grim Reaper dismissed him without probing further, I spoke up.

"Are we going to ignore that he already summoned at least one monster from the afterworld?" I queried. "Is it even legal for him to keep it as a pet?"

"No," Xavier said. "It's not legal, but the Council has never challenged him on it. I don't know why."

"The beast has been tamed," said the Grim Reaper irritably. "Hunt has never been involved in an attack on any innocent party. If he had, I would have taken action myself."

Reading between the lines, the beast *had* attacked humans in the past, but the Grim Reaper clearly wasn't budging on that one, and I admittedly couldn't think of any reason for Gwyn to kill Evan, his own apprentice. I'd have to let that one slide for the time being.

That left one person to question, both the most likely to

raise an objection to my involvement and also our main suspect.

After a long moment of silence, Val stuck her head through the doorway, her usual cheer notably absent. "Charon? Slight problem."

"Where's Freya?" asked the Grim Reaper.

"That's just it," said Val. "I can't find her anywhere. She's gone."

10

At the Grim Reaper's command, we split up to search the Reapers' house for any signs of Freya. It seemed a little pointless to me, given the Reapers' ability to search the afterworld in the space of a few seconds, but Xavier told me in an undertone that a Reaper of Freya's skill level might be capable of hiding herself even from other Reapers if she used the afterworld to cloak her presence.

It swiftly became apparent to all of us that there were no signs of Freya inside or outside the house. While any Reaper could have tracked her across town, the Grim Reaper flat-out refused to let any of the others leave the property and instead sent Xavier to pursue her while the rest of us waited in the house. While most of the Reapers returned to the meeting room, Val ignored the Grim Reaper's orders and joined me in the corridor to wait for Xavier's return.

"It seems unfair of Charon to make you stick around and wait," she remarked. "I did hear you telling him off earlier. That was brave of you."

I hoped the Grim Reaper didn't know she'd been listening

in. "I was just annoyed that he seemed to have forgotten this isn't my job."

"And yet here you are." Her mouth quirked. "I don't think Charon likes being reliant on a human, so he's coming down harder on you than he usually would."

"I wish he'd called the police instead." Maybe not, but at least the burden of playing the human investigator wouldn't entirely rest on me.

"I understand why he didn't," she said. "Now, if there was someone else reliable who wouldn't tell tales…"

"Not sure anyone exists, to be honest," I said, "much less someone who'll work for free for a bunch of secretive and rude Reapers right before Christmas… ah, I didn't mean you."

"I know I'm a thousand times nicer than the rest of them." She grinned. "That's why the others can't stand to be around me. Honestly, the feeling's mutual a lot of the time. It's so *dire*, the way they pretend that casting off one's humanity means abandoning any sense of fun too."

"Hmm." I wasn't sure I was supposed to be talking to her alone—she was still technically a suspect—but the Grim Reaper didn't seem to care, and I was starting to get a little concerned about why Xavier hadn't returned with our wayward Reaper in tow yet. "I hope Freya hasn't run away from town."

"If she has, that all but proves she's the guilty party," she said. "Though I can't think *why* she'd murder someone else's apprentice. Or set a monster on the loose that's more dangerous to the dead than the living. Seems out of character for her."

She didn't seem to have guessed that the beast had been summoned for the purpose of covering up a murder, but someone more paranoid than me might see her light tone as a cover for something less benign. I didn't really believe she had anything to do with this—Freya had all but declared herself the guilty party by running away—but I decided to change the subject a little.

"It looked as if it just went for my cousin and me because we happened to be there," I said. "Or because it was the only monster the killer had at their disposal at the time."

"Your cousin?" she asked. "I haven't met her yet."

"Trust me, you should be glad Cass wasn't the one pulled in here for questioning," I said. "She makes Lara look like a model of pleasantness."

Val laughed. "That makes me want to meet her more, not less. Out of curiosity, what were you and she doing out walking at night anyway?"

I hesitated for a moment, unsure if I trusted her enough to let her know, but I'd already told the Grim Reaper that Evangeline was spying on the Reapers' meetings, and it didn't sit right with me to keep that from the others. Besides, maybe talking to her would lead to some insights into their shared history that Xavier's boss would never divulge on his own.

"I was visiting the local vampires," I relented.

Her brows shot up. "I didn't know you could be friends with both."

"I wouldn't call us friends," I said. "Though most Reapers wouldn't call me a friend either."

"Better not say that in front of the others." She grinned. "I like you, Rory. You're honest."

"I don't think the Grim Reaper—I mean, Charon—would agree," I muttered. "They don't like each other much. Him and the vampires, I mean."

"I bet," she said. "I haven't had too many dealings with vampires myself since I'm new to the job. I thought I'd left all the posturing and petty grudges behind when I stopped being human, but apparently not."

"I guess people are all the same, living or... not." Maybe she wasn't the person to ask about the vampires' history with the Reapers, but there were other lines of questioning I could pursue. "Freya clearly has a chequered history with the vampires for different reasons than most Reapers, though. You knew?"

"It wasn't hard to guess if you asked the right questions." A wry smile came over her face. "The others didn't like my confronting her, but she wouldn't have given anything away on her own. She had Charon talking in circles for hours without anything close to a confession."

"Do you also think she killed Evan?"

"It makes no sense, but she's been acting more and more erratically the longer we've been here," she said. "She even wanted to summon that monster out of the afterworld last night, but Charon put his foot down."

"She was going to summon it back... Why?" I frowned. "I thought it wasn't the sort of beast that can communicate with people."

"It isn't," she said. "She said it might be able to lead us to the summoner. Since we're all Reapers, there's no trail of evidence to follow. Anyway, Charon said no. I imagine Reid banished that beast thoroughly enough that it won't be easy to call back. Janus will have taught him well."

"Really?" I asked. "Doesn't Janus have... ah, a reputation for unfortunate things happening to his apprentices?"

"Yes, but from the outside, it just looks like a streak of bad luck," she replied. "From what I've seen, Reid's determined to be the exception—not a bad attitude in an apprentice. Personally, I just picked whoever would be the most fun to be around for the next few hundred years."

"Is that really how long it'll last?" I asked curiously. "A few hundred years seems like a long time to be an apprentice."

Then again, an immortal might see such a centuries-long stretch of time to be nothing but a blink of the eye.

"It varies, but since I'm fairly new to being a Reaper, Alise and I will likely both be around a long while. We don't all follow the same timeline." She tilted her head. "Worried about that boyfriend of yours, are you?"

That hadn't been my primary thought, but it was difficult for me not to make comparisons to Xavier every time I heard another Reaper's story. "Not exactly, but his boss hasn't been forthcoming about how the whole thing works. When the apprentice takes over, I mean. That's how the Grim Reaper—Charon—started too? He was someone else's apprentice?"

"That's not always how it works, but an apprenticeship with another Reaper is the most common path," she said. "There aren't a lot of volunteers, as you can imagine."

"And when does the apprentice take over? When a Reaper… retires?" Retirement for an immortal didn't sound like something that should exist unless it was a euphemism for a grimmer fate.

"When they've had enough of the job. Or so I'm told." From Val's guarded expression, she'd realised that discussing such matters with a human might lead to a stern talking-to from her fellow Reapers, if not the Council.

"Reid told me that Reapers can be chosen from among ordinary people." I returned to the subject that held more interest for me than Reaper retirement plans. "That's not how it went for Xavier, though. He was pretty much born into it."

"So was Evan," she said. "But Reid and Alise both signed up willingly as adults. I think Lara did too, but Freya has never shared the details with us."

"Evan was born into the role?" I asked. "Gwyn took him in as a child, like Charon did with Xavier?"

"He's pretty close-lipped on the subject, but I got the

impression Evan was the child of a Reaper and a human, which is a union that the Council wouldn't allow. Generally, children from those relationships are swiftly taken into Reaper apprenticeships to avoid their skills with the afterworld being exposed to ordinary humans."

From what I remembered, something similar had happened to Maura before she left her apprenticeship behind.

"Isn't that dog of his also something the Council would disapprove of?"

She snorted. "Yes. Hunt is useful to have around, but the last time I tried to pet him, he nearly bit my hand off. He's definitely not a cuddly puppy."

"My cousin Cass would think he is, I bet."

"I'm liking your cousin more the more I hear about her, you know."

"I should probably find that worrying," I said with a reluctant smile. "I doubt you'll get to meet her, though. She isn't a fan of Reapers."

"Wise of her. I wasn't either, not before I joined."

"You weren't?" I raised an eyebrow. "Then why did you sign up?"

She paused for an instant. "I was already dying."

Whatever I'd expected to hear, it wasn't that. "You were?"

"I probably shouldn't tell you this, but it's hardly a big deal to me." She shrugged, a deceptively casual gesture that was belied by the absence of her usual smile. "I was injured in an accident and didn't expect to survive. While I was in the hospital, I was scared, and I knew the local Reaper, so I asked if I could sign up to join him. I thought it was going to give me time to say goodbye to my family. I was wrong."

"They wouldn't let you say goodbye?"

"I was pretty much dragged off for testing right away. I got a minute to say my goodbyes, and that was it. It's lucky I turned out to like the job, but it's not a career path I recommend choosing on a whim."

Whoa. The others might dislike her attitude, but she was plainly serious about her role. She'd sacrificed everything for the Reapers, even her family. "Was it worth it?"

"The job's got its perks," she said in a lighter tone. "The worst part was knowing my family will die of old age, while I'll stay around, unable to ever get close to them again. The job involves keeping others at arm's length, even your family. Not everyone can handle it."

No, I could never cut off my family. I was sure of that. "I couldn't, but I guess there's no chance the Grim Reaper would make any offer to me even if I was dying."

"It's not that common," she said. "Very occasionally, a Reaper will extend an invitation to a human who's on the verge of death, but that person wouldn't usually be in a good state of mind to make a decision that'll affect the rest of their life. In a manner of speaking."

I shivered. "Being born into it doesn't feel like a choice either."

"Oh, Xavier still had the choice," she said. "It wasn't that long ago that he formally accepted the apprenticeship. To be honest, we were all surprised Charon took an apprentice at all after he—"

The door to the meeting room slammed open, cutting off her words, and the Grim Reaper came sweeping out. "Where is my apprentice?"

"I don't know." I pressed a hand to my thumping heart. He'd scared the hell out of me. "Is he in danger?"

"No, but he should have returned by now," he said. "You will find him, Aurora."

"What?" I took a step back. "Are you ordering *me* to rescue *your* apprentice?"

"I will not leave this house while there are other Reapers present."

An objection rose on my tongue, but this was Xavier we were talking about. If he was in trouble of any kind, I had to find him.

I left the house at a run, reaching for my wand to transport myself to Xavier's side, but a loud commotion from nearby told me his location without any spells being needed. *Oh, no. Not there.*

I sprinted out of the cemetery and followed the sound of shouting up the high street to the vampires' house. A crowd had gathered outside to watch two individuals facing off against one another: Freya wielding her scythe against Evangeline, whose fangs were on full display.

And Xavier was positioned right between them.

"Xavier!" His name came out in a squeak. "Get out of the way!"

"Rory." He glanced over at me as I began to push through the crowd to reach him. "Stay back."

"I don't think so." I reached the front and addressed Evangeline first since she was usually the more reasonable of the two. "What's going on?"

"She was trying to sneak into my home," snarled Evangeline. "She used her Reaper powers to get in."

Uh-oh. I swivelled back to Freya, who didn't lower her scythe. "Why did you do that?"

"Because you have a number of criminals imprisoned inside this house," Freya said to Evangeline, completely blanking me. "I wanted to talk to them, and I knew you would not permit me to enter otherwise."

"My prisoners have not left the jail since they were incarcerated," Evangeline growled back.

"I think she might have found out that we questioned

them last night," I whispered to Xavier. "And she wanted a word with them herself."

A vampire–Reaper standoff was precisely what I'd been trying to avoid when I paid Evangeline a visit, but I could hardly believe Freya had willingly drawn a human audience. Whatever her intentions, the Grim Reaper had just lost all hope of keeping the drama among the town's disembodied visitors from the public at large.

"Did my boss send you?" Xavier whispered back.

"Seems he was worried." I faced Freya and raised my voice. "You don't want the Grim Reaper to come here to fetch you in person, do you? In front of all these people?"

Evangeline spoke. "Yes, I think Charon ought to handle this. However, I have not forgotten your transgression."

In answer, Freya lowered her scythe and turned away, vanishing into the afterworld. Several gasps and screams came from the humans gathered around, but when Evangeline also vanished into her house, the panic began to die down.

"I hope she *did* go back to the house," I murmured to Xavier.

Xavier's gaze drifted into the distance in the manner of a Reaper looking into the afterworld. "She did. We'd better go too."

The crowd gradually dispersed as Xavier and I walked away from the vampires' house. I slid my hand into his and whispered, "I was worried about you too. They might have seriously hurt you or worse."

"I was more worried for the humans watching, to tell you the truth."

"Yeah." That was yet another strike against her, and Xavier and I opted to walk back to the Reapers' house on foot in the hopes that some of the Grim Reaper's fury would dissipate by the time we got back.

We were in luck. The frigid temperature in the meeting room indicated he'd lost his temper with her, but his manner when he watched us enter was quite calm.

Freya, seated on the other side of the table, said nothing and didn't look at us either. When Xavier and I took our seats, the Grim Reaper began.

"You were caught breaking into the vampires' house," he said, "at the precise time you were supposed to be questioned in connection with an incident last night involving an after-world beast being set upon two humans. Were you trying to avoid the questioning?"

"I was not," she said. "I expected you to take longer to question the others than you did."

"And why did you visit the vampires?" he went on. "You must have known the risk you ran by confronting them publicly."

"I told you that I believed them to be responsible for Evan's death, and I still do."

"You didn't tell *us* that," I pointed out. "You thought the Founders killed him out of a desire for revenge on the Reapers? Where'd you get that idea—when you eavesdropped on us earlier?"

She gave me a cool look. "I will not apologise for the actions I took in defence of my own."

"I'm on the Founders' list too," I said, throwing caution to the winds. "It's very much my business. Besides, you put a lot of people in danger by trying to start a fight with the local vampires."

"I did not start the Reapers' feud with the vampires," she said coldly. "That rift has existed for millennia."

"Not today, you didn't," said Xavier. "But you must have Reaped at least one of their souls if you thought they'd want revenge on you. Am I right?"

She regarded him without emotion. "Yes, I did banish the

soul of one of their allies after he was killed in an accident involving one of their poisons."

Oh boy. "You didn't think to mention that earlier?"

"I was not aware that several of the Founders' allies were incarcerated in this town until earlier today."

Until she eavesdropped on us. This wasn't the first time she'd vanished and refused to give an explanation, though. Was she telling the truth? Someone who'd angered the Founders to that degree wouldn't have wanted to also earn the wrath of her fellow Reapers too, but there were still gaps in her story.

"Yet you decided to take matters into your own hands anyway," said the Grim Reaper. "If you believe that a vampire was responsible for Evan's death, how do you explain the attack on Aurora and her cousin last night?"

A heartbeat passed. "I cannot, but I can assure you I was not involved."

"We shall see," he said. "Until this murder is solved, you will not leave this house, or else you will be assumed guilty and pursued accordingly. Do you understand?"

I wouldn't have wanted to be Freya, pinned at the end of his punishing stare, but she remained undiminished. "This is a mistake, Charon, but I will comply."

And that was that.

11

"Who breaks into a vampire's house on purpose?" Estelle asked later, when I was back at the library. I'd just finished recounting the whole saga to the others, including the unexpected standoff between Freya and the vampires' leader in full view of the public. "Freya must have known she'd get caught."

"Maybe she assumed that being a Reaper would help her get away with it," I said. "I mean, they can walk through walls without making a sound. For most people, that's enough to evade attention."

"Except it'd be impossible for her to interrogate the prisoners without Evangeline finding out, given how sensitive vampires' hearing is," added Aunt Adelaide, who'd taken over desk duty for the day despite the lack of visitors. "Do you think she was telling the truth, Rory?"

"Hard to say," I admitted. "I can't think of any other reason she'd sneak around behind Evangeline's back. She strikes me as someone who usually follows the rules to the letter."

I didn't know what her apprentice thought of her behaviour, but I hadn't seen Lara that day. As soon as the Grim Reaper released me from questioning Freya, Xavier had escorted me back to the library to prevent his boss from roping me into doing him any more favours.

"It sounds like the Grim Reaper still has her listed as his prime suspect," Estelle said, "not the vampires."

"Freya disagrees, but I'm not sure her opinion matters that much," I said, "since, you know, the reason she sneaked into the vampires' home is because she eavesdropped on me and figured out there were a few Founders locked in Evangeline's dungeon. I don't know whether she genuinely suspected them of murder or was just trying to cover her own guilt."

"That's suspicious behaviour in itself," said Aunt Adelaide. "I wouldn't trust her word."

"I don't, but the Grim Reaper doesn't seem to be able to act against her without more proof or a confession," I said. "She's danced around giving actual answers for a day. I thought he was going to contact the Reaper Council for confirmation on her history of banishing vampires' souls, but he seems to have changed his mind."

"Why, because he thinks it'll make him look bad?" Estelle asked. "That he let someone get murdered in his house?"

"Must be." I shook my head. "The problem is there is no proof Freya *did* kill Evan. The Grim Reaper thinks that she summoned that monster to devour his soul before anyone could become aware of his death, but since the beast can't identify the person who called it out of the afterworld, they can only make guesses."

"And nobody has looked at Evan's body yet?" Estelle guessed.

"No." I heaved a sigh. "Every time I suggest calling in

Edwin or someone else, I run headlong into a brick wall of Grim Reaper stubbornness. He won't bend."

"Doesn't the person whose apprentice actually died get a say in this?" said Estelle. "You'd think he'd want to know the truth."

"Gwyn?" I thought back to the other apprentices' discussion immediately following Evan's death. "The Grim Reaper doesn't seem to think so, and he's the one calling the shots. The only people who outrank him authority-wise are the Council. If they *did* show up in town, they'd call for a more in-depth investigation, but that might cause more problems than it solves."

Not least when it comes to my relationship with Xavier. It would be difficult for the Grim Reaper to explain the events following the murder without admitting he'd allowed his apprentice to bring a human into the Reapers' confidence, and it might well be him who paid the consequences for enabling our relationship. If he feared the wrath of his leaders, it might explain why he'd treated me like even more of a liability than he usually did, though it didn't make his behaviour any less annoying.

As for the others, maybe it was too much to hope that the other Reapers would ever accept Xavier and me as we were, not as long as we remained severed: Reaper and human.

Val's warning lingered at the back of my mind. No, I didn't want to join the Reapers and lose my family in the process, and my conversation with Reid yesterday had been a stark reminder that even casting aside my human life was no guarantee I'd get to keep Xavier as my own. If Xavier would be torn away from me one way or another, there seemed to be no winning, but Val had made it clear that becoming a Reaper was an irreversible decision, one I wouldn't be able to turn back from.

"Rory?" Estelle saying my name brought me back to earth.

"You aren't thinking of looking at the body yourself, are you?"

"I—" I hadn't been, but it wasn't the worst idea. "I'm not sure I'm far enough in my magical training to be able to identify any poison or spell as the cause of his death."

"A simple revealing spell would expose any magical cause," Estelle said. "You don't need to know precisely what it is."

"Don't give her ideas," Aunt Adelaide said. "You've done enough for the Reapers without any thanks, Rory. You'd give the killer another reason to target you again too."

"Yeah, don't do that," said Estelle hastily. "The Reapers are way more durable than you are. It's not worth it."

Don't remind me. "I don't know what else to do."

Before the words had left my mouth, the front door opened, and the Reaper apprentices entered the library. Reid came in first, followed by Alise and Lara then a very apologetic Xavier.

"Hey," said Alise brightly. "I know you're open today, so we thought we'd come and have a look around."

My mouth parted. "Do your bosses know you're here?"

"Obviously," said Lara in a bored voice. "They gave us permission to come. I didn't really care, but I'm sick of the sight of that house. I doubt this will be any more exciting, but whatever."

That's nice. I could see that even Estelle was struggling to keep her friendly manner in place as she and my aunt greeted our visitors.

Xavier leaned over and whispered, "Sorry. I told them not to come, but I figured you wouldn't have many visitors today. I hoped it wouldn't be too much trouble."

"Of course not," I murmured back. "I'd be happy to give them the tour."

Some of them, anyway. Lara made to walk away alone,

shunning Estelle's invitation to join us, but the sound of beating wings above brought her to a halt.

"Ooh, who's this?" Sylvester landed on the desk, peering at the new arrivals with his large owl eyes. "I spy three Reapers."

Reid jumped in surprise, and even Lara took a step back. Only Alise was unperturbed.

"Hey, you have a talking owl," she said. "I've never met one of those before."

"I am far more than an owl," said Sylvester imperiously. "I am a superior being."

Lara gave an incredulous snort. "Is this a circus or a library?"

Uh-oh. Sensing the need to step in, I said, "This is Sylvester. He's our familiar."

"Familiars can't talk," Lara said then took another step back when Sylvester raised his wings outward so that he took up three times the space.

"Let me give you the tour." I stepped between the pair of them. "Sylvester, I'll show them around the library."

The owl huffed while Lara turned to walk away. As she did so, he sent a gust of air into Lara's back, making her trip over a trapdoor that had silently appeared near the front desk.

The trapdoor in question led to the basement containing the vampire who'd been sleeping in the library for decades without any of us even knowing his name. I cast Sylvester a warning look. While it was amusing to imagine Lara getting a close-up encounter with our fanged housemate, I wouldn't put it past her to report everything she saw here straight to her boss. Whether Freya was the killer or not, I didn't want her coming within a metre of the library if I could help it.

Sylvester got the hint, luckily, and Lara stepped over the trapdoor without falling in. Aunt Adelaide watched with a slight smile as if she'd half considered pushing her into the basement herself. I didn't blame her, and I was unsurprised when Lara barely lasted a minute into Estelle's tour of the lower floor. She declared the whole library to be a boring waste of time and retreated to the Reading Corner. I sent Jet to keep an eye on her in case she wandered through one of the locked doors and rejoined the others.

"Miserable, isn't she?" Alise gave her fellow apprentice a pitying look. "She's trying to hide how terrified she is that her mentor's going to be locked up in the Reaper Council's jail."

"Is that likely?"

"No, because Charon won't hand her over without iron-clad evidence." She spied a collection of books floating above the shelves and ran over to watch them circle like a flock of birds. "How're they doing that?"

Discussing the murder investigation swiftly became impossible as the library was replete with distractions, and I answered Alise's stream of questions the best I could while keeping an eye out for any troublemakers, owl-shaped or otherwise. Sylvester had wisely opted to leave Lara alone, and she remained sulking in the Reading Corner until we called her to join us up on the first floor. Then Lara gave an irritable snort and got to her feet as if she'd been invited to clean out a room of manticore dung rather than on a tour of a magical library.

She kept up a steady mutter of complaints all the way to the stairs, and when Estelle asked if anyone had any questions, she said, "Why do you have two Christmas trees?"

"Why not?" Estelle's tone was free of her usual character-istic cheer. "It's the holidays."

"It's garish." Lara gave a haughty sniff and climbed the stairs with her nose in the air.

"You weren't kidding," Estelle said to me in an undertone.

"She makes Cass look pleasant. Speaking of whom, I kinda hope she'll come out of her room."

"Not sure I agree." The Reaper apprentices already outnumbered the other visitors we'd had that day, which at least meant that I could give my full attention to the tour and prevent anyone from wandering into any corners that we'd prefer to keep away from the public.

Luckily, most Reapers at least had the courtesy not to walk through the walls while inside someone's home, even Lara. She did display a little curiosity when we passed by one of the padlocked doors marked 'Do Not Enter' and again when we neared the Dimensional Studies Section halfway between the second and third floors, but she avoided that pitfall, and we made it around the first two floors without any incidents.

At the second floor, I found myself at the back of the group with Reid. Come to think of it, I still hadn't thanked him for saving my life. Nor had I revisited the subject of our first conversation while I'd been showing him around the town the previous day. Of all the Reapers I'd met, he was the one who'd most recently joined them on the other side of the grave, and I found myself curious as to what had gone into his decision. A relationship couldn't have been the only factor, surely.

"I never thanked you for what you did for me earlier," I began, "for saving my cousin and me from that monster."

"No worries." He certainly *looked* worried, glancing around as if afraid that same monster would jump out from behind a bookshelf and attack us.

"What's wrong?" I asked.

"Can I talk to you alone?" he murmured. "It's important, but I can't say any more in front of the others."

"Okay." Unease skittered down my spine as I led the way behind a row of bookcases until we were out of hearing distance of our companions. "Tell me. What's going on?"

He halted, his gaze travelling along a row of books instead of meeting my eyes. "The truth is… I think I know who the killer is."

My heart missed a beat. "What? Who is it?"

"It's—" He choked off. "It's Janus."

"Your supervisor?" That couldn't be right.

"I saw him… I saw him with that monster. Inside the afterworld." He shuddered. "He was communicating with it somehow, but he sent it away when he realised I was nearby."

"Communicating with the monster?" I sucked in a breath. "You don't think *he's* the one who summoned it?"

"He must have," he said. "I don't know why, but I know what I saw."

"Why would he summon something that can't kill anyone who's alive?" I tested the waters, reasoning that he wouldn't have any reason to know of the conclusions that Xavier and his boss had drawn unless he'd been thinking along the same lines.

"Because it can devour spirits," said Reid. "If the person who summons the beast is particularly skilled, they can direct it to consume someone's soul as soon as it's removed from the body, before any other Reaper even senses their death."

He figured it out too. "You mean… Evan."

"Exactly." An urgent note entered his voice. "If my master summoned that beast again, he must plan to use it against someone else."

"Why Evan, though?" That much, I didn't get. "Why target an apprentice in the first place if not his own?"

"I don't know." He chewed on his lower lip. "But I wonder if it might be why his last apprentices died. Maybe he got the wrong one this time."

I opened my mouth and closed it. His conclusion might be understandable, given his position, but there was still little logic to the idea that Janus would strike against one of the apprentices while at a summit with four other Reapers within watching distance and at the Grim Reaper's house, no less. Something didn't add up.

"If it's true, we need to tell someone," I said, "before anyone else gets hurt."

"There's no proof," he said. "That's the problem. Janus can walk into the afterworld and talk to the monster without anyone being any the wiser. He's a powerful enough Reaper that nobody else can track him unless they already know he's there."

"Then we can tell them what to look for," I said. "We can trust Xavier and his boss."

"No," he insisted. "They'd let something slip before he could be locked away, and—and you know that the first person he'll target is me."

His fear made sense, and while part of me remained sceptical of his master's guilt, letting this go without telling Xavier was out of the question.

"How can we expose him, then?" I asked. "Short of catching him in the act, that is, and that's only possible if that monster shows up again. Or if he sends it after someone else."

"He might," he murmured. "If he's guessed that I'm onto him, he'll want to tidy up the loose ends. And... and I did wonder if he set that monster on you last night because he planned to do the same as he did to Evan."

"I wasn't alone, though. I was with my cousin."

"I didn't mean to worry you," he added, "but I think we can take him by surprise if we're careful. He'll try to call that monster back as soon as he thinks he's not being watched."

"In the afterworld," I said. "Only a Reaper can track him. Right?"

"The others won't believe me if I go alone," he said. "But— I can take you with me. As a witness."

I shook my head instinctively. "No way."

"Haven't you been in there before?"

"I have, but it's not exactly something the Grim Reaper approves of." How did he even know? "And I certainly can't break the rules with four more Reapers in the house who don't think I should even be involved in this."

I'd been into the afterworld with Xavier countless times, but I trusted him, and besides, even a Reaper apprentice ran the risk of falling afoul of the monsters lurking on the other side.

"I'll let you think about it," he said. "I know it's a lot. I just… Please don't tell the others."

"I can tell Xavier," I said. "I *should* tell him. I bet he can help you, and he won't report us."

Reid lowered his gaze. "If you're sure."

I looked for Xavier and spied him near the shelves, watching the pair of us as if wondering what we were talking about. Bracing myself, I walked to his side, but before I could say a word, a clamour of voices arose from nearby. One was Lara's, and the other voice distinctly belonged to Aunt Candace. *Oh no.*

"What's going on?" I asked Xavier.

"Your aunt followed Sylvester up here."

"Please tell me she isn't questioning Lara about Reaper business." Not that Lara didn't deserve it. Hoping the others could handle them both, I seized the chance to beckon Xavier closer. "I—and Reid—need to tell you something."

"Sure." He blinked, his attention shifting to Reid as his fellow apprentice stepped out from behind the shelf. "What were you two talking about?"

"Reid told me that he thinks his boss is the killer."

Xavier's mouth thinned. "How did he figure that one out?"

"He saw Janus talking to that monster in the afterworld," I explained. "But he doesn't want to tell the others yet in case he's the one who takes the punishment for it. Given his mentor's track record, I can sort of see where he's coming from."

"Yeah." He paused for an instant. "We'd have to be careful. If Reid's telling the truth, Janus is dangerous. Does he know Reid suspects him?"

"No, but if Janus *is* the killer, his apprentice's word might not be enough. He needs someone else to act as a witness. In the afterworld."

A shadow fell over his face. "He wanted to take you into the afterworld with him."

"Obviously, I'm not going in there without you," I reassured him. "The thing is, he needs a witness to be there who isn't one of the suspects."

"I'll go there instead."

I should have known he'd say that. "You don't think the others will think you're biased too? Since you're also an apprentice?"

"They might, but my boss will believe me, and that'll be enough," Xavier said decisively. "If Reid is right, I'll go with him into the afterworld, and we'll catch his boss in the act before anyone else gets hurt."

12

B efore anything else, we had to finish the tour, which was made significantly more challenging by Aunt Candace's and Sylvester's attempts to torment our grumpiest visitor. Eventually, Lara tried to get away by fleeing into the Dimensional Studies Section and ended up sliding around in all directions for nearly ten minutes before Estelle was able to rescue her.

Aunt Candace watched the show, cackling the whole time, while Aunt Adelaide and I took charge of stopping Alise from trying to open various cabinets and picking up books that objected to being manhandled. When one leather-bound tome started emitting a siren-like wail that set off a chorus of shrieks from its neighbouring books, I offered to escort her to the front desk.

Reid and Xavier both waited for us there, having caught up on Reid's plan to catch his boss in the act of summoning a monster. Reid spoke somewhat tersely to Xavier; probably, he wasn't happy with me for letting him in on this, but leaving Xavier in the dark was out of the question even if it meant sitting on the sidelines myself while the pair of them went into the afterworld without me.

When we finally left the library, Reid let the others overtake us and spoke to Xavier and me in an undertone. "My boss will know I'm on my way back to the house with the others. It'll be easier to catch him out if we go directly to him through the afterworld from here."

"And when we find him?" Xavier asked. "What then?"

"We banish the monster and then go straight to someone who has the authority to have him arrested," I said more decisively than I truly felt. "So, your boss."

Of course, that was assuming two apprentice Reapers would be a match for a fully qualified one, with or without a lowly human present. What if they were walking straight into a trap?

"I want to come with you," I told them. "I know I don't have to come *into* the afterworld, but if anything goes wrong over there, I can tell the Grim Reaper where you are. It won't hurt, will it?"

Xavier's mouth parted, indicating he wanted to argue, but I was starting to have second thoughts about my resolution to stay back. While regular magic didn't work inside the afterworld and there'd be little I could do to help, the notion of letting Xavier go off alone with Reid gnawed at my conscience. Yes, Xavier was a far more experienced Reaper than Reid was, but what if it wasn't enough? What if the pair of them couldn't subdue Janus and that monster alone?

I watched the other apprentices for a moment. Lara stalked ahead, while a cheerier Alise attempted to make conversation with her and was rebuffed. When the pair vanished behind the cemetery gates, Xavier and Reid were ready. They checked nobody was watching, and together, they lifted their hands in unison and called upon the afterworld.

Darkness swept in, swirling around the pair of them. Reid vanished first, and as Xavier stepped into the dark, I impulsively took his hand. He stiffened but didn't shake me off, and a heartbeat later, we were gone.

All light and sound faded, to be replaced with absolute darkness quieter than anything that existed on Earth. Through some sense that wasn't available to humans, Reapers were able to map that dark place onto the real world beneath and use it to traverse impossible distances, but to me, the dark expanse looked the same no matter which direction I turned. No ground existed beneath our feet, and the usual laws of physics were shaky if not nonexistent. I didn't even need to breathe though I found myself taking in quick breaths and gripping Xavier's hand tightly. At least I could still see *him*, albeit in a less solid form than he usually was.

Reid, too, hovered on the spot like a ghost, scanning the darkness for his mentor. Another ability Reapers possessed was a kind of sixth sense that enabled them to track a particular individual within the afterworld if that person was someone they knew well, and within heartbeats, a window opened in the air. The darkness folded outward like a pair of curtains on the world, revealing an equally dark area in which there stood the hooded figure of a Reaper, stooped low next to the shaggy form of a monster.

The Reaper's head began to turn in our direction, and the dark curtains slid over the window again, hiding us from his sight.

"That was him." Reid's voice trembled a little. "Do you believe me now?"

"That was definitely Janus?" The figure had been in full Reaper mode, without any features that made him easily recognisable to my human eyes, but the pair of them would be able to identify him easily.

"It was," Xavier confirmed. "He didn't see us, but we'll need to get closer."

"Are you sure his Reaper senses didn't pick up on us?" I spoke in a whisper.

"I don't think he was paying attention to anything but that monster." Reid lifted a shaky hand. "I can try to hide us, but he's a better Reaper than I, and he might see through the ruse."

"I'll help." Xavier, too, lifted a hand, and a kind of shroud materialised in front of the three of us.

Then a second window opened, this one much closer to the tall Reaper and the great shaggy monster. From this angle, I recognised something of Janus in his stance, his height maybe. He didn't move—but the beast lifted its head and looked directly at us.

Reid stiffened. The veil-like substance in front of us swayed then disappeared as the beast growled, treading closer.

"Leave," Xavier said to the beast. "Now."

The Reaper had also noticed the intrusion, but at a gesture, Xavier opened a second doorway in the air, this one directly beneath the monster. At once, the shaggy beast fell, letting out a piteous wail as it vanished deeper into the dark.

"Janus." Reid stared through the area where the monster had been, directly at his boss. "You summoned that beast, didn't you?"

Janus didn't answer for a moment. Though he didn't have his human face on—no need for that here—it was clear that we'd startled him. "Apprentice, you misunderstand."

"Master, I saw you," Reid said, his voice trembling a little. "I saw you speaking to that beast earlier, and now two other witnesses have seen the same. I won't let you hurt anyone else."

"No." A louder, more chilling voice echoed throughout the gloom. "You will not."

My blood turned to water. I watched as the Grim Reaper glided into view, his attention fixed on his fellow Reaper.

"Charon," said Janus. "These apprentices have misunderstood my intentions."

"Your actions were clear to me." The Grim Reaper raised a hand, and the afterworld peeled away, revealing the meeting room beneath, as if the darkness had been an illusion the entire time.

The other Reapers, seated at the table, stopped midargument and surveyed Janus with some surprise. Freya and Gwyn were swift to school their expressions back into impassiveness, but Val goggled openly at him.

"Explain," said the Grim Reaper. "Now."

"I called upon that beast to take me to its summoner," said Janus. "My apprentice simply misunderstood the situation."

"Summoning beasts from the afterworld is against our laws," said Freya. "The Council forbids it."

"It's also common practise." Janus gestured at the formidable form of Gwyn's hunting dog leaning against the table. "As some of us know. I wanted to get answers."

"Forgive me if I do not believe you."

As the others began to fire off their own accusations, I leaned closer to Xavier. "You told him?"

"Of course I did."

I'd thought the Grim Reaper would want the pair of us to stand at the centre of the questioning as we had before, but he'd seen enough of Janus's actions himself that he seemed content to ignore us. Aside from asking me to confirm what Xavier had already told him, Xavier, Reid, and I were all but pushed out of the discussion and left forgotten.

"He doesn't expect your boss to buy his excuses, does he?" I whispered to Xavier when Janus uttered another stream of protests. "How often do Reapers call monsters out of the afterworld for non-illegal reasons?"

"More than they should, according to my boss," Xavier said back. "It *is* possible to convince an afterworld beast to lead you to its summoner, if you know what you're doing. But Janus knew the Grim Reaper forbade them all from trying to contact that monster after Freya suggested doing the same thing."

"What'll they do to him?" I asked.

"The Council will deal with him, I expect," Xavier said. "He'll be put on trial."

"He will." The Grim Reaper looked directly at us. "I will talk to Aurora and my apprentice alone for a moment."

A shiver raced over my skin as I followed Xavier out of the room and into the corridor. The instant the door closed, the Grim Reaper turned on his apprentice.

"I thought," he said, "I told you not to bring Aurora with you into the afterworld."

"I was there as a witness," I protested. "Isn't that why you wanted me involved in the first place?"

"There was no need for you to be there, not in the afterworld."

"Reid thought his master would kill him if he reported him without any proof," I argued. "I'd say that's a good reason to have as many witnesses as possible."

"Do you wish to testify to the Council?" The Grim Reaper's voice gained the sort of echo that reminded me of the dark expanse we'd left behind, a place of no light or joy. "They will come here, and if your involvement is discovered, the consequences will be severe."

"For me or you?" Dread coiled at the base of my spine. "Wouldn't that have happened anyway, no matter who turned out to be responsible? *You're* the one who called me in as a witness as soon as Evan was murdered. I didn't volunteer." *Not at first, at any rate.*

"My fellow Reapers know that you were in the afterworld, Aurora," he said. "If not for that, I may have been able to conceal your involvement, but now, you have made a difficult situation infinitely worse."

"What does it matter?" Xavier said. "There's a criminal in that room right now. You should focus on punishing him, not blaming Rory for helping us."

"You cannot get away with any of this behaviour when you are a full Reaper," he said to his apprentice. "I've been too lenient on you. You forget what you must become, and that day will arrive before you know it."

I backed up against the wall, body swaying as if caught in a gale-force wind. A quiet, rational voice in the back of my mind told me that the Grim Reaper's words were a cover for his own fear of suffering the consequences for all the times he'd bent the Council's rules—but his words struck home, drawing up the worries that had been brewing in the back of my mind since my conversations with the other Reapers.

You cannot get away with any of this behaviour when you are a full Reaper.

But when was that? When *did* he plan to retire? Had he and Xavier ever discussed the subject? And when the Grim Reaper hung up his scythe for good, what would that mean for us?

The Grim Reaper swept back into the meeting room, beckoning his apprentice to follow. Xavier cast me a remorseful look but dared not disobey, and as he vanished into the room, Reid stepped out into his place. "Rory, are you going home?"

"The Grim Reaper kicked me out." I feigned nonchalance and turned to the front door. "It happens."

"After you risked your life to help?" He followed me on swift feet. "I'll walk back with you. It's only fair."

I half wanted to tell him to let me walk alone, while another significant part of me wanted to confide in the only person whose situation even came close to the one that Xavier and I found ourselves entangled in. While Reid's story hadn't had a happy ending, who else would understand?

"Doesn't the Grim Reaper need to ask you more questions?" I asked him, closing the door behind us.

"He doesn't need anything else from me either," he said. "I already gave my report, and Charon thinks Xavier is less biased than I am because he's not apprenticed to Janus and he's also far more experienced as a Reaper."

"And I'm human." The past few days had been a painful lesson in how little that meant.

"That doesn't make you any more unreliable than the rest of us," he said. "We were all human once. And Xavier is your boyfriend. That's no insignificant commitment for either of you."

I blinked hard, glad of the cold air to make my stinging eyes easier to hide. As we left the cemetery, I forced out the words "What you said about your decision to join the Reapers… How long did you get with her? The person you loved? Before she had to leave?"

"A year." He lowered his gaze. "She never came back. When I took the apprenticeship, she'd been gone for two years."

That meant the other apprentices who'd died must have come in during that short interval.

"Why did she choose to leave town?" I asked. "I know you said she went to take another Reaper's place, but she could have said no, couldn't she?"

"Not to Janus." He kept his eyes on his feet, his expression pained and disarmingly human. "He might have regretted sending her away when he had so much trouble keeping an apprentice afterwards, but when a Reaper retires, they need to find an immediate replacement, or else a lot of souls get lost with nowhere to go. Someone had to volunteer to step in."

"Does that mean you're… you're going to take his place now?" Hadn't he only been training for three months? Was that enough time to reach the level of a fully qualified Reaper?

"I…" He trailed off. "I could quit, technically, but that would leave the region without a Reaper at all."

"You're allowed to quit?" I frowned. "I thought it was forbidden."

"It's not encouraged, but it sometimes happens," he said. "I don't know how common it is. To be honest, my experience is limited to my own region. I've only been doing this a few months, and this was my first annual summit."

"What a way to start." I tried for a light tone, and he gave me a reluctant smile.

"I know," he said. "But it's the first for you too, I bet. You weren't at last year's summit, were you?"

"No." *A year.* Xavier and I had been together just under a year. What if that was all we had?

"It was cruel of Charon to keep you away." When I blinked in surprise that he'd guessed, he added, "I figured it was something like that. Am I right?"

I blinked hard. "It's nothing. Really, don't worry about me. You're the one dealing with a far bigger problem."

"Considering that until recently, I thought I might be killed by my own master, it could be much worse," he said wryly. "Anyway, Charon has a reputation for being hard on his apprentices, or so I hear."

"Apprentices?" Had that been a slip of the tongue? My mind drifted back to my conversation with Val earlier, which the Grim Reaper himself had interrupted, and curiosity drove me to ask, "Was there someone else before Xavier?"

"Ah." He gave me a sideways look. "I don't think Charon would be happy that I know this, but my master mentioned he briefly took on another apprentice a long time ago."

"The Grim Reaper trained someone else?" My mouth fell open. "I… I didn't know you could have a trial and then quit."

"You can," he said. "Being a Reaper is a major commitment, not one that anyone will say yes to, even while on the brink of death. In fact, that's probably the worst time to make the decision. Jumping in without thinking about the consequences first is a disaster waiting to happen."

Who would have said no to the Grim Reaper? "Did you know who it was?"

"Well…" He fidgeted with his sleeve. "I heard a name. I'm probably not supposed to share it, but I guess it doesn't matter since the person is already long dead. Audrey Hawthorn."

Hawthorn.

I knew that name. I'd heard it before… at the library.

Grandma.

Shock blanked out my thoughts. Grandma—had trained as a Reaper?

"Here." Reid's voice cut through the fog in my head.

I realised that I'd been so wrapped up in our conversation that I hadn't noticed we'd reached the library. I was scarcely conscious of saying goodbye and opening the door or of stumbling inside.

"Rory, did you catch the Reaper?" Estelle asked anxiously. "You didn't do anything dangerous, did you?"

"No. Yes, but it doesn't matter." I attempted to marshal my scattered thoughts. "We caught him. I don't know what the Grim Reaper's going to do next. He threw me out before I could ask."

"Threw you out? After you helped him?" Estelle said indignantly. "I hope that's the last time you ever offer him a favour, Rory."

Tears pricked my eyes. "I'm sure the Grim Reaper would prefer that."

She wrapped me in a hug. "Ignore him. Your part in this is done now, isn't it?"

"I should hope so," said Aunt Adelaide. "You found the killer, didn't you?"

"It was Janus." The story spilled out of me in a rush. When I came to the end, I had to reveal the final bombshell. "Did you know Grandma was briefly an apprentice Reaper?"

Aunt Adelaide stiffened. "My mother did what?"

"Reid told me," I explained. "Grandma briefly signed up for a—a trial or something, but I guess she backed out."

I was assuming Reid had been honest with me, but why lie about something like that? Moreover, it made so much more sense that the Grim Reaper had been badly disposed toward me from the start. Not only had my dad been a perpetual thorn in his side, but I was also a reminder that his last apprentice had quit.

Did Xavier know? Had the Grim Reaper told him about his failed predecessor, or had he concealed the truth like he had from my family and me?

"When was this?" Estelle's eyes rounded.

"I have no idea." The Grim Reaper alone knew the details, and he'd give up his scythe before he shared them with me. "Probably years before he took on Xavier."

"That makes no sense," said Aunt Adelaide. "My mother would never have…"

"She would," Estelle said, sounding half doubtful, half awed. "We all know the level of secrets she kept from us in plain sight. Maybe she did have another second life that none of us knew about."

"Maybe." Aunt Adelaide chuckled disbelievingly. "I suppose she spent enough time upstairs on the fourth floor that we wouldn't have noticed she was gone."

"And it explains why the Grim Reaper doesn't like our family much," I said. "Aside from my dad and I being an endless source of trouble."

"I didn't know Reaper apprentices could quit," said Estelle wonderingly. "I thought it was a job for life."

"So did I, but everyone signs up in a different way," I said. "Val signed up when she was already dying. That would be harder to reverse."

A thought slid into my mind. If the Grim Reaper had extended the same offer to my dad, would *he* have said yes? If we'd been able to say goodbye… But Dad would have given up his life rather than existing in the half life of a Reaper. Even Grandma had done the same in the end.

Being a Reaper didn't give you more time with your loved ones. You couldn't fix old mistakes. All you could do was exist somewhere between death and beyond, never able to truly belong to the living again.

I might have called it a kindness that the Grim Reaper wanted me excluded from that kind of life, but that didn't make his dismissal hurt any less.

13

Aunt Candace's reaction to finding out about Grandma's secret sojourn as a Reaper's apprentice was to vanish up to the fourth floor all afternoon. Just when we were ready to send a rescue party, she returned covered in dust and wearing a scowl. "She wouldn't tell me."

"Who's 'she'? The guardian?" I ducked as a pile of notebooks came soaring overhead, accompanied by floating pens busy scribbling notes in each of them. "How many novels in progress did you get out of this? Five?"

"Seven," she said, vanishing into the living quarters in a swirl of ink and paper.

At least sharing ideas with my family about Grandma's secret history was a temporary diversion from the upcoming visit from the Reaper Council, but the matter was rarely far from my thoughts. Even if the Grim Reaper didn't tell tales on me himself, did I really expect the other Reapers to avoid mentioning my excursion into the afterworld to their superiors? Freya's grudge was bound to have multiplied tenfold now that she'd been proven innocent after suffering the indignity of being accused of a crime by a human, but would she want to risk the Council's wrath by putting herself in the spotlight?

After an eventful family dinner involving Aunt Candace trying to bring all seven of her notebooks to the table, Estelle and I sat in the living room, drinking hot chocolate, while another winter storm raged outside. It would have been a nice, cosy scene if not for the lingering threat of Reapers hanging over our heads and the knowledge that the library had once again hidden a world-shaking secret right underneath our noses.

"Do you think we should ask the fourth-floor corridor ourselves?" said Estelle. "About Grandma being the Grim Reaper's apprentice, that is?"

"I don't think we'll have any more luck than Aunt Candace did." I blew on my hot chocolate to cool it down. "The guardian can't talk either."

"True, but Grandma might have left a record behind somewhere up there. I can't believe even my mum didn't know."

"This must have been years ago, before either of us was born."

"I can believe it." Wonderment filled her voice. "She must've worked hard to keep it quiet. She'll have been working full-time in the library and raising my mum and Aunt Candace at the time."

"If she spent as much time in her room as Aunt Candace does, I can see why nobody noticed," I remarked. "In fact, maybe that's what Cass does all day."

"Cass training as a Reaper?" She snorted. "Nah. She hates going outside unless it's to retrieve a magical animal."

"I think she'd have fun walking around with a giant scythe." The mental image was amusing enough to cheer me up a little, if nothing else. "I know she wouldn't abandon her animals."

Not many people would willingly leave all their loved ones in that way. Even Xavier had done so because he hadn't had anyone to miss… at least until he met me. Did he know how long he'd stay in the role before his boss retired? Was I reading too much into the Grim Reaper's claim?

I drained the dregs of my hot chocolate as if the warmth would banish the chill deep inside me. While Estelle went to refill our mugs, I stared out the window at the rain and pondered on why Janus had seemingly risked so much to kill another Reaper's apprentice. Maybe Reid was right and he'd been the intended target himself, like his predecessors had, but the question of why a Reaper would want to kill the person they were supposed to be training to succeed them lodged in my mind like an itch that wouldn't go away. Everyone who'd worked for Janus had seemingly met the same fate, except for Reid's former girlfriend—

I jolted in my seat when I spied a pair of giant owl eyes watching from the darkness above the sofa.

"How long have you been lurking up there, Sylvester?" I tilted my head toward him. "Did *you* know Grandma was briefly employed as a Reaper's apprentice?"

"Why on earth would I, you feather-brained lawnmower?"

"You seem to know all about everything else that goes on in here." I spoke mostly to appease him, though it struck me that Grandma had also been the one who'd overseen his creation when she turned the library from an ordinary building into a sentient place possessed of its own will.

"I do hope you mean that as a compliment." The slightly threatening note to his voice prompted me to shuffle out from beneath the cabinet in case he dropped more tinsel on my head.

"I did, and I really want to know."

"Want to know what?" Laney descended the stairs with her usual silent grace, having awakened for the night.

Since Sylvester didn't seem inclined to answer, I said, "Supposedly, my grandmother had a brief stint as a Reaper apprentice."

Laney's eyes widened. "She did? What else did I miss?"

"That isn't even the half of it." I recounted Reid's confession and our excursion into the afterworld and finished up with the Grim Reaper's dismissal and the subsequent addition to the already convoluted tangle of my family's history.

"You caught the killer," she said. "At least there's that."

"I've also guaranteed us a visit from the Reaper Council for the holidays," I said. "And it'll be a small miracle if the Reapers get through their interrogations without giving away that they let a human into their business."

"The Council ought to make an exception, considering you helped them stop a traitor in their own ranks." She pursed her lips. "Does Evangeline know you caught Janus in the act?"

"Not yet." I hadn't had the will to pay her a visit and enlighten her, and not because that monster might come back and attack us again. If Janus was indeed the culprit, the danger it posed was minimal, but I had to wonder how the Reapers were planning to keep him contained until the Council showed up to arrest him. That he'd been able to summon that beast in the first place told me that he was practised at sneaking around in the afterworld without any fellow Reapers sensing what he was up to. From what I'd gathered, Reapers could hide their actions from one another if they were on equal footing power-wise, but that made his temporary imprisonment seem less than secure. The other Reapers would be watching carefully to make sure he didn't escape before the Council showed up.

Estelle walked back into the living room with a fresh mug of hot chocolate in each hand. "Hey, Laney. What—*ahh!*"

She dropped both mugs when a dark figure dramatically materialised in the middle of the room, his shadow blotting out the dim lamplight. Laney sprang back with a hiss, and even Sylvester took flight from the cabinet, his wings clipping the back of my head.

"Grim Reaper." I took a step back, my heart racing in my chest. "What is it? Nobody else died, did they?"

"My apprentice is missing," he said. "I assumed he was with you."

"What do you mean, *missing?*"

"He isn't in the house," he said." I've checked the afterworld, and he's untraceable, which suggests he's in the library."

"He really isn't." A thousand questions crash-landed in my head. "In the library? Are you sure he isn't somewhere else in town, hidden from sight?"

"No, he isn't," he responded. "I would be able to sense his presence. Either someone else tried to conceal him, or he's in here."

"It can't be Janus, can it? You locked him up." I looked toward Laney and Estelle, who seemed equally baffled. "Are you implying that you can't sense Xavier when he's inside the library? Not at all?"

"I cannot." It sounded as though it pained him to admit it. He'd never told me before that he lost all awareness of his apprentice's location while Xavier was here in the library, but if it was true, it would explain why the Grim Reaper had initially been so resistant to his apprentice spending so much time here. "There was one other time in which he disappeared from my awareness. Recently."

Laney's head snapped toward him. "Let me guess. It was

when he was under the effects of that potion. You lost track of Xavier then too?"

No way. "You didn't tell me that."

"At the time, I was not aware he was in any danger. I assumed him to be in the library." His sightless stare bored into me. "It took some time for him to tell me the full story of how he was captured by that vampire, and when he did, I realised that the potion must have concealed him from my sight."

Cold sweat dampened my palms. When Xavier fell under the effects of the potion, we'd brought him to the library immediately to administer a cure. If the library itself also made him untraceable, then the Grim Reaper hadn't known he was under the effects of the potion until Xavier himself had told him so.

"Shaw Senior didn't say if anyone else had access to those potions." My mouth went dry. "He might not have known, but Carlos Verdant never answered all our questions."

"I'll speak to—" Laney cut off when he vanished as swiftly as he'd arrived, leaving a Reaper-shaped impression on the inside of my eyelids. "Evangeline."

"Dammit." I looked at Estelle, who stood ruefully over the spilled hot chocolate. "I'm sorry. I'll help you clean up."

"Never mind that," Estelle protested. "Xavier is missing? How can that be?"

"It's the Founders again." I turned back to Laney, adrenaline surging in my veins. "We should go and find Evangeline before the Grim Reaper is the next person to start a fight on her property."

"Agreed."

"No chance." Cass stepped into the doorway to the living quarters, her arms folded over her chest. "I knew you were going to sneak out again."

"You know vampires are more active at night, don't you?" I nodded to Laney. "Anyway, Xavier is missing."

"And you think the vampires are responsible, do you?"

"The Grim Reaper does, and I don't want to see another Reaper–vampire standoff any more than you do."

Cass shadowed Laney and me to the door. Before opening it, I reached for my umbrella, but Cass lifted her wand and conjured up a transparent shield in midair between us and the rain. Then she stepped pointedly outside, wearing a defiant expression as if daring me to tell her to go away. I made a mental note to ask how to cast that spell and followed her and Laney into the night.

We passed by the cemetery without stopping, the dark night concealing the Grim Reaper's house from our field of vision. If I hadn't been so worried for Xavier, I might have tried to work the situation to my advantage and to get him to promise to let us spend the holidays together, but right now, I'd have happily taken on the Council itself just to see Xavier's face again. Nothing else mattered.

I saw no signs of the Grim Reaper outside the vampires' home. Evangeline opened the door before either of us could knock.

"I have already told that wayward Reaper I've seen no signs of his apprentice," she said in irritable tones. "Was there any need for *three* of you to come?"

"Are you sure those prisoners of yours aren't hiding something?" I queried. "The other Reapers are all accounted for, but Xavier… He's gone."

"Perhaps he has come to his senses about the life prospects involved as an apprentice Reaper."

Her words struck me like a slap. "Excuse me?"

"She's right, you know," said Cass.

"That's not helping," Laney shot at her, to my surprise. "You know that potion Shaw Senior was brewing? The Grim

Reaper admitted that it concealed Xavier from his Reaper senses."

"He told me the same, with great reluctance," said Evangeline. "That does not mean any of my prisoners was able to attack the Reapers."

Chills raced down my spine. "If one of the Founders *is* behind this, I find it hard to believe that the prisoners don't have at least some awareness of what they're up to."

Yes, Laney had read Shaw Senior's mind and confirmed he had no idea who else might have access to those potions, but Carlos Verdant had tried to scare us off rather than answering our questions, and it was he who'd brought a Reaper into their ranks.

Evangeline's eyes narrowed. "I see that you are not to be deterred. Very well, Aurora."

When she beckoned us into the house, Laney glided ahead, but Cass hovered on the threshold. "I'll wait outside. I doubt the prisoners will talk if we all march in there at once."

Her tone suggested she still thought this was a waste of time, but it wasn't an argument she was going to win. Nor would Evangeline, though she wore a disapproving stare as I accompanied Laney to the stairs and we once again descended into the vampires' dungeon.

The prison cells looked even more forbidding without any daylight streaming in from above, though it was Shaw who shrank away from Laney when he saw us approaching his cell. "What do you want this time? I thought you were done with your questions."

"Not quite," I said. "That potion you used on Xavier. Someone else had access to it, didn't they?"

"Who wants to know?"

"We do." Laney appeared inside the cell behind him. He jumped off the bench with a yelp, but she seized the back of his shirt and stopped him from squirming away. "I've no qualms about staking you. I've done it before, and if anything, I think Evangeline will thank me for it."

The little colour left in his face drained away. As a new vampire, newer even than Laney, Shaw knew he was on the losing side.

"I don't know," he mumbled. "Really, I don't. I didn't give the potions I made to anyone else, but when Vale showed up, he criticised me for not making it strong enough. That's all he said."

"What does that mean?" Laney demanded. "Stronger than knocking a Reaper out cold?'

"Strong enough to kill." A rush of lightheadedness swept over me. "Like…"

"Like the poison used on vampires. If the dose is too high." Laney let go of him and reappeared at my side, her hand taking my elbow before I sank to the floor.

A scream lodged in my chest, but I swallowed it, forcing myself to breathe calmly. If Vale had had others brewing the same potion, anyone else might have gotten their hands on some. It didn't mean that was how Evan had died—someone reaping his soul with a scythe would have left no mark on him either—but his body had been left behind in the Grim Reaper's house. Xavier, however, was nowhere to be seen. And if the Grim Reaper had already searched the house and found no signs of him, where could he be?

A cold laugh resounded in the darkness. With a snarl, Laney ran toward Carlos Verdant's cell, her fangs bared.

"Stop!" I sprinted across the darkened room, only to slam headlong into Evangeline. I stumbled back, clutching my throbbing head. Faint light streamed downstairs, revealing that Evangeline held Laney by the scruff of her neck, preventing her from reaching Carlos Verdant's cell.

"I would ask you not to attack my prisoners," she said. "I have kept them alive for a reason."

Carlos Verdant laughed again. He stood at the front of his cell, his expression alight with amusement. "This is the most entertainment I've had since my incarceration began."

Laney fought to escape Evangeline's hold, to no avail. "You were in on this, weren't you? This supposed feud with Vale was just a cover. You were both working on the same thing."

"We had our differences, yes, but you are correct that we have always worked toward the same shared goal." A cruel smile tilted his mouth. "We seek the preservation of knowledge and of our eternal lives. There is no greater threat to our aim than the Reapers. They must be eradicated."

"I suppose targeting all the other vampires who disagree with you doesn't count." Laney freed herself from Evangeline's hold, her voice thick with loathing. "If you know who's behind this, Verdant, I'll kill you."

"He did not." Her eyes gleamed dangerously. "You will find the person responsible for this, Elaine, while I see to Verdant's punishment myself."

"It better be a good one," Laney growled.

"Come on." We didn't have time to argue. I needed to find the person who'd used that potion before Xavier met the same fate that Evan had.

14

Cass, still waiting outside, reacted with little surprise to the knowledge that the vampires had been at the root of this murder.

"Of course they were," she said. "Between them and the Reapers, it's a wonder any of us made it to the year's end."

"Some of us didn't, or not in the same state we started in," Laney said. "Don't worry. I'm still alive enough for this."

"I—" Cass sounded uncharacteristically hesitant. "Sorry. That was unfair."

"Don't worry about it." Laney waved a dismissive hand. "What's the plan? Search the Reaper's house for clues about where Xavier's kidnapper took him?"

"The Grim Reaper already looked and found nothing." I walked away from the house, rain creeping in around the edges of the shield Cass had conjured over our heads.

"Only because he didn't look hard enough," said Cass. "Xavier's unconscious body has probably been shoved into a cupboard somewhere."

"Okay, *that* wasn't cool," said Laney.

"Don't argue," I said over my shoulder as I strode downhill as fast as my human legs could carry me. "Come on."

When I knocked on the door, the Grim Reaper greeted me with his customary faceless glare, which intensified when he spotted Laney and Cass behind me. "Why are *they* here, exactly?"

"To help search the house," I told him. "Look, we know Xavier is probably unconscious somewhere, and if he can't be tracked through the afterworld, we'll have to turn this place upside down to find where they put him."

"You assume I have not done so myself?" said the Grim Reaper. "Since Janus was taken into custody, I took it upon myself to assign Xavier to watch him from inside the afterworld. To my knowledge, he has never returned to the human realm."

"You think Xavier's still in the afterworld?" My chest tightened at the thought of Xavier in the afterworld, unconscious and alone. "We have to get him out of there."

"And how do you propose to do that, Aurora?" said the Grim Reaper. "He cannot be tracked by anyone, and if I am unable to find him, nobody can."

"I beg to differ." Cass spoke up loudly. "You might be a master of death, but you're not the best at everything, and the person who took your apprentice targeted your weakness. I bet someone who isn't a Reaper can find a way."

"How?" I caught sight of someone else behind the Grim Reaper: Reid, beckoning me into the house. "Let us in. You asked me to help, didn't you?"

The Grim Reaper glided aside to allow enough space for me to enter but stopped short of letting the others follow me.

"Is it true?" Reid met me on the other side of the door. "Xavier is missing?"

"Apparently so." My hands curled into fists at my sides. "When was the last time you saw him?"

"His boss took him upstairs to the room where they locked Janus. I assumed he was being put on security duty."

"He was." *In the afterworld.*

Might Reid be able to help? If even the Grim Reaper couldn't track him down, there was no way an apprentice could do the same, but Reid was more likely to let me come with him than the Grim Reaper was.

"I can't sense him," said Reid quietly. "And the others can't either. He's outside of our awareness. I worried that… that it means he's like Evan."

Fear knotted in my chest. "He's not. I know he isn't."

"Then how is he hidden from us?" he asked. "What can best a Reaper?"

That potion. The trouble was the killer might have disposed of the evidence via magical means without leaving a trace at all. There was no guarantee that searching the house would do anything but wear away at Xavier's already limited time.

"Let me know how I can help," Reid pressed. "Charon hasn't let us help with the search, but if there's anything you need me to do…"

Take me into the afterworld. I swallowed my request. The Grim Reaper would never allow it, and besides, Reid was only an apprentice. If we ran into something too dangerous for him to deal with, we'd be trapped alongside Xavier—or worse.

"Where are the other apprentices? Still in the living room?" I asked instead.

"That's right," he said. "Our bosses are in the meeting room, and Charon hasn't let anyone leave."

Who would have had the means to attack Xavier, then? Something in Reid's manner suggested that he knew what I wanted to ask, but caution urged me to resist. "Xavier was upstairs… Is that where Evan's body is?"

If any proof existed indicating that Evan had been dosed with the same potion that had been used on Xavier, it would be there.

"Must be," Reid said. "I didn't see Charon take his body out of the house, so it must still be in here somewhere, and he hasn't let any of us go upstairs since Evan died."

Raised voices in the doorway prompted me to turn around to check on my cousin and Laney.

"What's a vampire in the house compared to a murderer?" Cass was saying to the Grim Reaper. "If you can let *me* in, you can let her in too."

"I will not allow any vampires into this house."

"Cass isn't a vampire." Though I suspected that wasn't the problem. "Cass, I need your help. Laney, you don't mind waiting outside?"

"Of course I don't," Laney said impatiently. "Don't argue on my account. Find Xavier."

"Cass," I said when my cousin didn't budge, "c'mon."

"I have rescinded my offer," said the Grim Reaper, "given your cousin's overt disrespect towards myself and my fellow Reapers."

"Disrespect?" I echoed. "Get over yourself."

If I hadn't felt my own mouth move, I might have thought the words came from Laney or Cass instead of me. I'd spoken as though possessed, without conscious thought. My nerves caught up with me a heartbeat later, but the Grim Reaper said nothing at all.

"If you'd let someone look at the body in the first place, we'd have figured out how Evan died sooner." Again, the voice sounded like mine, but it spoke without input from my brain, straight from the well of anger and frustration that had been bubbling inside me over the past few days. "Now, your apprentice has been taken by the killer, and you already admitted you can't get him back alone. Are you going to let us help you, or is your pride worth more than Xavier's life?"

Silence rang out. My heart jackhammered against my ribs as my nerves finally caught up with the enormity of what I'd said. Neither of the others spoke. Cass's mouth twitched into a smile, while Laney gawked openly at me.

"What," said the Grim Reaper, "do you propose we do instead?"

For some reason, the calmness in his voice disarmed me more than anything he'd said so far. "Let Cass and me look at the body. Evan's body. We can go from there."

I didn't know what the next step would be, but I needed to get out of his line of sight before I pushed him over the edge and wound up with a scythe in my back.

The Grim Reaper spoke to the others. "Cassandra, you may enter, but only you."

"Fine." Cass walked past him without seeming to care when her arm brushed against his hooded cloak in a manner that would have shoved him aside had he had a physical body. Reid began to speak, but Cass stilled him with a wave of her hand. "Go away. We can handle this."

Reid obeyed, scurrying out of sight, and I shook my head at her. "Cass, now is not the time to antagonise everyone. We need to find Evan's body."

"What's the point in that?"

"The potion." I lowered my voice. "If the killer used it on him too, it'll give us a trail to follow."

"That's the easy bit." She tapped her coat pocket, inside which I could see the outline of her Biblio-Witch Inventory. "It'd be easy for us to track Xavier if he wasn't out of our reach, wouldn't it?"

"It's somewhere to start." I paced ahead down the hallway. "I don't know which room Evan's body is in, but I think he's upstairs."

Cass made a sceptical noise but overtook me and began climbing the stairs.

"Wait." I hurried to catch up to her. "I don't know which room the Grim Reaper locked Janus in, but we don't want to walk in there instead."

"He put some kind of Reaper defences on the door." Reid glided upstairs after us. "Let me find the right room. It's safer."

"Didn't I tell you to go away?" Cass tested a couple of doors then tried one that caused her to drop the handle with a hiss of pain. "This'll be Janus's room, then."

"Are you all right?" I gasped when I saw her hand was blistered all over as if she'd picked up a red-hot frying pan.

"It's cold, not warm. Feels weird." She winced, fumbling for her wand with her other hand, and cast a spell that caused a bubble to appear around her injured palm. While the blisters healed, Reid tried more door handles until he found one that wouldn't give.

"This one." He pushed on the handle again. "It's locked but otherwise harmless."

"Right." Cass lifted her wand again and cast an unlocking spell, causing the door to open so violently that Reid nearly tripped over the threshold into the room. "Now, go on. We can take it from here."

I flashed him an apologetic look as I ran after her. Evan's body was laid out on the floor, as cold and pale as when we'd found him two days prior.

"Let's find out how he died." Cass crouched beside the body and waved her wand, revealing a stream of bright-pink light hovering above Evan's face. The light illuminated faint splatters against his pale skin, transparent enough that even a Reaper's eye might not have picked up on them.

"The killer did use the potion on him."

I ran my finger down the list of words inside my Biblio-

Witch Inventory, lingering over the one I needed. *Find.* In order for it to work, I needed a clear mental image—but I'd never seen the potion up close, and a few transparent splatters weren't enough to conjure up an accurate picture.

If Xavier had been in this realm, the same spell would have taken me directly to his side, but we were literally worlds apart. *And yet...*

An impulse seized me, and I pressed my fingertip to the word *find.* I pictured Xavier's face, focusing on the image and squeezing my eyes shut so that I could pretend he was standing right next to me. Gritting my teeth, I dug my fingernail into the page so hard that my hand trembled.

Sudden ice-cold air flooded the room. Cass swore, and my eyes flew open, taking in the improbable sight of a window opening in midair and revealing a pit of darkness on the other side.

The afterworld. I'd opened the *afterworld.*

"What have you done?" Cass waved a frantic hand at the unnatural apparition floating in the middle of the room. "Get rid of it."

"I don't know how!" I flipped through the book, but there wasn't a single word in there that included *closing doors to the afterworld* in its definition. "I don't know how I even did it."

Had anyone ever tried using their Biblio-Witch Inventory to open the afterworld before? Grandma had trained as a Reaper—but she wasn't around to answer any of our questions, and we had bigger problems at hand. A growl sounded from within the darkness, and a monstrous shaggy beast appeared in the window, its dark eyes scanning the room.

"Now look what you've done!" Cass backed away until she reached the doorway into the landing. "Rory, get away from that thing!"

"Go!" Reid came running into the room, shouting at the beast. "Get out of here!"

The beast fled at his command, leaping through the open doorway and into the darkness beyond. Then he ran to my side. "Rory, how did you do that?"

"I don't know." Words tangled in my throat, the urge to ask him to close the doorway warring with the certainty that I'd been able to open it precisely because Xavier was somewhere on the other side.

"How?" Reid closed in behind me, staring at the book in my hands. "What is that?"

"My family's magic." I leaned closer to the doorway, trying to spot any traces of Xavier within the dark. "Xavier's in there."

All I needed to do was step through the door—but if I did, would I be able to get out again? What if something worse than that monster waited on the other side?

"Then we'll get him out." Reid reached out to take my hand and let out a yell as a flash went off behind us. Cass stood pointing her wand at him, her mouth twisted in anger.

"No, you won't," she warned. "Get away from my cousin."

"Cass, wait—" My cry was cut off when Reid shoved me over the threshold of the doorway, into the darkness waiting on the other side.

15

"Reid!" I spun around, adrift in darkness without solid ground beneath my feet, as the last traces of the real world vanished entirely.

"Sorry, Rory." Reid's voice drifted after me, through a window that was no longer there.

It was him. It was all him. The realisation hit me in the same instant that it sank in that I was trapped in the same realm as a soul-eating monster.

I held up my Biblio-Witch Inventory like a shield as I rotated on the spot, taking in the darkness pressing against me from all angles. Reid had ordered the monster to leave, and its easy obedience made it obvious that he'd been the one who'd summoned it in the first place. He'd been playing me from the moment we'd met, using my relationship with Xavier as a route to gaining my trust, and now—

Xavier. He was somewhere in here, and I'd been trying to find him when I'd done the impossible and opened a doorway to the other side. He must be close, but I didn't have a Reaper's ability to sense any person in the afterworld, and Xavier was hidden even from the Grim Reaper. Still, knowing he was nearby helped me to put a lid on the panic threatening to overwhelm me. Xavier might have been within my reach, but in his current state, he was in as much danger as me, if not more. *If that monster comes back...*

I shut down the thought and held up my Biblio-Witch Inventory, taking comfort from the fact that it didn't appear any different in here than it did in the world of the living, except that it was as transparent and insubstantial as my physical body appeared to be.

Did that mean I could use magic in the same way? I'd always thought otherwise, thought that no other magic worked in the afterworld at all. And I didn't particularly want to think of what fate awaited a human left in the after-world for an extended period of time. That monster was still out there, and if it brought a friend that did have a taste for living people rather than ghosts, I'd be dead before I breathed the air of the real world again.

I opened my Biblio-Witch Inventory, but the words wavered before my eyes as my panic returned.

Focus, Rory, I told myself again. I'd already opened a door into this realm, and the library itself was also a place that defied all usual dimensions. I had to believe it could help me get to Xavier—and get us out.

I ran a fingertip down the page and tapped the word *find,* again picturing Xavier's face in my mind's eye and focusing on that image with all that I had.

The darkness spun around me. My head whirled, and I closed my eyes to dispel the dizziness, gripping my Biblio-Witch Inventory in both hands.

My arm bumped against something solid. My eyes snapped open once again, and a gasp escaped me. Xavier hovered suspended in the air, his eyes closed, his body unmoving. Terror gripped me. "Xavier!"

No response—he was completely under the effects of the

potion, and his hand, when I took it, was as cold as the grave. He couldn't open a way out of the afterworld, not like this. The sight of him so helpless rattled me beyond words. While I knew I had to get us out of here, it was little more than an accident that I'd got here to begin with. I had no idea how to get out, let alone how to bring someone else along for the ride.

He's a Reaper. You can do this.

I held up my Biblio-Witch Inventory in my free hand, my other grasping Xavier's, and raised both of our palms to the exposed page. One word leapt out at me. *Travel.*

"Please work," I murmured, my fingertip brushing the page. It was hard to hold the book one-handed and keep it on the right page at the same time, not without letting go of Xavier, and my finger kept sliding over the word. I released Xavier's hand and moved closer until our bodies were pressed against each other, side by side. Then I lifted the book again and tapped the word *travel,* focusing all my attention on a mental image of home, of the library.

The afterworld gave way, the darkness folded outward into a window in the air, and we toppled down, down, into the real world.

We landed with a thud that shook my vision into a thousand fragments. I lifted my head, registering Xavier's solid body lying beneath me, icy air filling my lungs, and the shock of sudden cold rain pouring over my head. We were outside, lying on the ground outside the library. That must have been the image my Biblio-Witch Inventory had latched onto when I'd brought us out of the afterworld.

"Xavier." I gently shook him, but he didn't budge.

The library's door opened, and Estelle came running out. "Rory!"

"Help him." I lurched to my feet, pushing a handful of

soaking hair out of my face. "Oh, no. I left Cass and Laney at the Reapers' house."

With a murderer. Reid... What if he'd hurt Cass too? She'd been trying to get him away from me, but she'd been too late, and nobody in the house had had any idea that he was working against them.

Estelle leaned over Xavier's body. "What's wrong with him?"

"That potion." From outward appearances, I couldn't tell if he was alive or dead. He didn't have a pulse nor a heartbeat nor any breath in his lungs—but if he was dead, Reid wouldn't have seen the need to leave him in the afterworld beyond reach. *Right?* "I'll come back and explain as soon as I can, but I left Cass in the same room as a killer."

Estelle sucked in a sharp breath. "I'll take care of him, but please, Rory—"

I was already running away, my feet pounding on the hard stone as I left the library behind. It was lucky I'd brought us here and not to somewhere unfamiliar to me, but Reid had already been alone with the others for long enough, and nobody else in that house knew him for the killer he truly was.

Upon reaching the cemetery, I pushed open the gate and ran into darkness so dense that I didn't see Laney hiding behind a tombstone until she appeared in front of me.

"Whoa." I skidded to a halt and would have fallen onto my rear if she hadn't taken my arm to steady me. "Laney, what's going on in there?"

"How did you get out?" She released my hand, turning back to the shadowy form of the Reaper's house. "I don't know what's going on in there, but I saw that apprentice, Reid. He came running out of the house, looking seriously shifty. I was going to chase him, but I thought you might need my help in there."

"He's the one who used the potion on Xavier and trapped him in the afterworld." Fear coiled inside me. "And—he was with Cass when I last saw him."

"What?" She ran back to the house and reached for the door, cursing when her hands bounced off the wooden surface as if she'd met with an invisible shield. I hadn't known that the rule about vampires needing an invitation to enter someone's property was quite *that* rigid, but outright panic spread across her face as she pounded at the invisible barrier. "We have to get her out of there!"

"I can get in." I knocked, but the fact that Reid had been able to flee unopposed suggested that Xavier wasn't the only Reaper he'd used that potion on. When nobody answered, I pulled my wand out and cast a spell that knocked the door open onto an eerily empty hallway.

"Help her." Laney's voice sounded choked. "I was so mad at her earlier, but I know she came here for my sake, and I should have said something to her sooner."

"I'll find her." I ran past the living room door, which was slightly ajar. Lara and Alise both lay unconscious on the other side. Reid hadn't trapped them in the afterworld like Xavier, but he hadn't needed to hide proof of what he'd done, not this time.

The meeting room door was closed, and I held my breath as I pushed it inward.

On the other side, three Reapers lay sprawled beside the table: Gwyn, Freya, and the Grim Reaper—but not Janus. He was still imprisoned, perhaps unaware of anything else going on in the house. Or maybe Reid had used the potion on him, too, to ensure nobody would challenge him. Like—

Cass. I backed out of the room and made for the stairs, hurrying up to the room in which I'd last seen Cass. The door was closed, but a loud thumping sounded from within. Heart in my throat, I cast an unlocking spell.

"That scumbag!" Cass exploded as she burst out of the room. Her hands were bright red and bruised, suggesting she'd been banging on the door the whole time she'd been in there.

"You're all right!" I gasped. "I thought he killed you."

"He's too much of a coward," she said. "All he did was lock me in here, right after he pushed you into the afterworld. How in hell did you get out?"

"The same way I got in." I tapped my coat pocket, where I'd stashed my Biblio-Witch Inventory. "I'll have to figure out what that means later. The other Reapers are all unconscious, and Reid has run off."

"And—Laney?" Her voice caught on the last word. "Where is she?"

"Outside. She couldn't get in, and she's worried about you too."

Cass pushed past me and ran for the stairs. I descended behind her, chilled by how unnaturally quiet the house was after the noise level of the past few days.

Laney waited at the door, where I'd left her. When she saw Cass, her worried expression melted into relief. "This vampire invitation thing is bloody annoying sometimes."

"He didn't hurt you." Cass paused as if unsure what to say next.

For a moment, they stared at one another, and while I wanted to give them some privacy, we didn't have time to sort through their feelings and misunderstandings with a killer still on the loose.

"I'm going after Reid," I said, and both of them started then hastily looked away from one another. "I left Xavier at the library, but the others are worried about you, Cass. Someone needs to let them know we're alive."

"I'll come with you," Cass said. "Laney—you run to the

library and tell the others I'm all right. You can catch up to us more easily."

"But…" Laney trailed off, presumably seeing the logic in her suggestion. "Fine."

She disappeared in a blur of vampire speed while I took out my Biblio-Witch Inventory again. This time when I tapped the word *find*, I pictured Reid's face.

I'd half expected another doorway into the afterworld to open, but instead, we landed in an ordinary street lined with houses. Reid—who must have fled the mundane way instead of via the afterworld—came to a startled halt when Cass and I appeared in front of him.

"Rory?" He took a step back, gaze darting around in panic. "I can explain."

"Don't you even think about doing a runner." Cass tapped on her own Biblio-Witch Inventory, and his body left the ground, flipping upside down in midair. Even that wouldn't have stopped him from opening a door to the afterworld and escaping, but rather than fighting, he tried to meet my eyes, his expression pleading.

"What did you do to Xavier?" I demanded. "To the others? Are they dead?"

"No, I just knocked them out. They aren't dead." His mouth trembled. "I didn't want to hurt anyone."

"You killed Evan."

A flush crept over his upside-down face. "An accident. He caught me smuggling the potions into the house, and I panicked. I only meant to knock him out."

"A likely story," Cass said. "You're a murderer, and you summoned that monster of yours to cover your tracks so that none of the Reapers would sense his death."

"It was a mistake," Reid said, a touch of desperation in his voice. "I was trying to *save* him. The other apprentices too.

They're trapped, same as me. The Reapers treat us like scum, keeping us from our families, our loved ones..."

"Is this all about that girlfriend of yours?" I asked. "The Reapers stopped you from being with her, even after you joined their ranks, so you decided to take revenge? Wait—are you the one who killed Janus's previous apprentices too? Because you wanted the job for yourself?"

"I..." He avoided my eyes, and I knew I'd guessed right.

"You did all this for a girl?" Contempt dripped from Cass's voice. "You *killed* other apprentices? And you think we'd believe you're out for anyone but yourself?"

"That potion." My thoughts went back to my last visit to Evangeline's dungeon. "You must have known it can kill in a high dose. Didn't the Founders tell you that?"

"The Founders?" He continued to hover upside down, caught in Cass's spell. "I got the potion from... from another Reaper."

"When was this?"

"Couple of months ago."

The Reaper who was working for the Founders. She must have sold him the potions before she got caught.

"I really didn't want to hurt Xavier," he added, "but he kept asking questions, and I had no choice but to put him somewhere he wouldn't give me away. I didn't plan to leave him in the afterworld forever. As soon as I explained the truth to you, I was going to help you both leave town, leave the Reapers."

"What?" I gave a disbelieving laugh. "Are you kidding me?"

"Isn't that what you wanted?" he asked. "I saw that it was tearing you apart, having to choose, so..."

"So you decided to make the choice for me? For both of us?"

I was a little surprised at how steady my voice sounded,

but I'd passed the point of shock long before, and all that was left was rage.

He must have seen something in my face, because he chose that moment to break free of Cass's spell and vanish into the afterworld.

"Get back here!" I knew what to do now. I lifted my Biblio-Witch Inventory and tapped the word *find*, once again picturing Reid's face in my mind's eye.

As before, a doorway opened in the air. Reid, hovering amid a sea of darkness extending beyond my field of vision, gave a double-take when he saw me. I reached through the doorway to grab him, but my fingers passed through empty air. The doorway began to close, and I withdrew my hand, reaching for my Biblio-Witch Inventory again.

Cass got there first. As she tapped the page of her own book, a window opened in midair, this one directly above our heads. Reid came tumbling out, landing in a heap on the pavement.

"Don't you dare!" She reached for him, and he twisted away, another doorway in the air opening above the road.

Before he could leap in, Laney came sprinting into view. In a heartbeat, she had Reid in a headlock, her fangs brushing the skin of his neck.

"I've never bitten a Reaper before," she said. "I expect you taste pretty terrible."

"That won't work." Reid twisted, trying to free himself, inching closer to the doorway he'd opened.

"Go in there, and I'll pull you out." Cass tapped her Biblio-Witch Inventory with a finger. "Face it, we've got you trapped."

"Where are we supposed to lock him up?" I whispered, gripping my own Biblio-Witch Inventory. "Does the library have a room that can keep him contained?"

"We're not taking him to the—" Cass broke off with a

curse. "Oh, fine. I'm sure taking him there won't cause problems at all."

"Xavier's already there." And we'd need to visit the fourth-floor corridor to get a cure for the others too.

"You're making a mistake," Reid said desperately. "I'm trying to help you, to help everyone."

"Save it." Cass sounded bored. "C'mon. Let's bring him in."

A closer look at my surroundings told me we were still in Ivory Beach. He hadn't gone far at all, and it was a simple matter for Cass and me to use our Biblio-Witch Inventories to transport all four of us back to the library's doorstep.

When I opened the door and saw Xavier was with the others, my knees went weak with relief. "You're okay."

"Rory." He wrapped me in a hug. "I hoped you hadn't gone far."

"Did Estelle wake you up?" I released him, eyes stinging with relieved tears. "We can do the same for the others."

"What about…?" He trailed off, spying Laney and Cass approaching, the former hauling Reid along by the back of his shirt.

"We caught him," I explained. "We need to keep him contained until the others wake up."

Assuming they do wake up. That was the problem. If the Grim Reaper died—really, truly died—what would happen to Xavier?

16

The half hour that followed was among the most nerve-wracking of my life. Xavier had recovered from the effects of the potion, but the other Reapers remained comatose, and there was no efficient way to transport four Reapers and two apprentices to the library without drawing attention from the locals, especially when our prisoner might easily give us the slip if we left him unattended.

"Sylvester might be able to help us secure him," said Aunt Adelaide, clearly thinking of the Forbidden Room. "Sylvester!"

"He's not here." Aunt Candace came out of the living quarters in a tornado of notebook pages. "He told me in no uncertain terms that the next person to ask him to help deal with a Reaper-related problem will be turned into a permanent ornament on his tree."

"The fourth-floor corridor, then?" I dropped my voice to a whisper in case the owl overheard and decided to turn me into a bauble anyway. "Seriously, the longer those Reapers stay unconscious, the less chance we have of reviving them before Reid does another runner."

"Maybe we should lock him in a cabinet as an exhibit," Aunt Candace said. "You know, we don't have decisive *proof* our magic doesn't work on Reapers. We can just keep trying every word in our inventories until something works."

"Not helping!" Estelle ran past, attempting to restrain a book that had sprouted a large number of tentacles. "The library doesn't like him being in here either."

"The afterworld is always an option." Aunt Candace's smile was positively ghoulish. "I would *dearly* love to know why our much-lamented mother decided not to tell any of us that our magic has the capacity to affect the afterworld as well as this one."

"Speak for yourself," Aunt Adelaide said through gritted teeth, taking aim at the tentacled book with her wand. The tentacles withdrew, allowing Estelle to put it down, but intermittent shrieks and crashes from upstairs told me it was far from the only book that had been disturbed by the intrusion. We couldn't keep Reid in here for long.

"We need the other Reapers," I muttered to Xavier, who'd been able to do little but stand and watch the chaos unfold. "I'll try to get the cure to them while you and Cass keep an eye on Reid."

Cass was currently on guard duty outside the room where we'd locked him, but we'd only made him stay put under threat of one of us pulling him straight out of the afterworld again as soon as he tried to escape. At some point, he'd slip through our clutches, and I didn't much fancy the idea of chasing him through the afterworld from right here in the library.

Needless to say, the others had been stunned to learn that the ability to open the afterworld had been at our fingertips the whole time. Since Grandma, nobody had had any reason to make use of that talent though I was kind of concerned as to what Aunt Candace might get up to. It didn't surprise me when Aunt Adelaide swiftly laid down a new rule: "No opening the afterworld in the library."

"I only wanted to take a look!" was Aunt Candace's disgruntled reply.

"Our mother would never have wanted us to use that talent here unless our lives were in danger," Aunt Adelaide said. "If I ever see you breaking that rule, I'll ask the library to confiscate your Biblio-Witch Inventory myself."

It was at that point that I'd felt the prickle of unseen eyes on the back of my neck. When I looked up, I spied the guardian lurking on the stairs, its shadowy form similar enough to a Reaper's that I had to wonder if that was where Grandma had got the idea for its design. The guardian's presence had been enough to convince Aunt Candace not to try any more ill-advised experiments, and it was still lurking on the stairs when I made my way up to retrieve a cure for the other Reapers.

At the third floor, I sought out the brightly painted door that led to the fourth-floor corridor. Upon climbing the staircase, I found the correct door and pulled a pen out of my pocket. Then I pressed the tip to its wooden surface.

I wish for a cure to wake up the Reapers, I wrote.

The door opened, revealing a small room containing nothing but a table upon which lay a single bright feather, a phoenix's feather. Did the library have an infinite supply? Where had Grandma got them from? So many of my questions about this corridor were still unanswered, and though the guardian had tailed me upstairs, it didn't speak a word, not even to explain why Grandma had kept yet another world-shaking secret from her entire family.

I was halfway downstairs when a loud knock on the front door reverberated up from the ground floor. Heart pounding in my chest, I picked up speed and climbed down to the lobby.

A Reaper stood in the doorway, his hooded form tall enough to block out all light. "Where is my apprentice?"

"Janus." My heart jangled in my chest as I approached him. "I thought you were still locked up in the Reapers' house."

"I made my escape as soon as I realised my apprentice had turned on the others." He gestured to a large wolfhound at his feet. "Hunt assisted me, and we went to warn the Council of his treachery. However, by the time I escaped, I found no signs of my apprentice in the house."

"He's locked up in here." I pointed over my shoulder towards the empty room in which we'd shut him. "Xavier's watching the door."

"You were able to revive him?"

"Yes, and I can do the same to the others. You found them, didn't you?"

"I did, and that is why I summoned the Council. They're waiting at the house now."

The Reaper Council. He'd brought them to Ivory Beach. For an instant, my mind refused to accept it, too overwhelmed with everything else that had happened today to accept that the scenario I'd been trying to avoid for months might be on the brink of becoming a reality.

"They'd better not come near the library." Cass marched into view with her arms folded over her chest. "They aren't welcome in here."

"I came alone." He glided across the lobby until he reached the door outside which Xavier stood. His stricken expression indicated that he'd overheard enough to know that the Reaper Council was already present in Ivory Beach.

"I have the cure." I held up the feather between trembling fingers. "You can take it back to the house yourself."

Janus ignored both of us and opened the door to his apprentice's prison. I heard Reid's gasp on the other side. "Janus. I…"

"You have committed crimes, apprentice, and will be punished accordingly."

"Wait." Xavier took a step toward the door as Janus and his apprentice vanished into a swirl of darkness.

"Great," Cass said. "Now we're going to have Reapers thinking they can open the afterworld in the library wherever they like."

"I thought you didn't want him here." Laney sounded more amused than anything.

Something in their dynamic had shifted since we returned to the library, and I'd seen them whispering to one another in the brief periods of stillness amid the chaos of locking Reid in the spare room and deciding what to do next. Based on how close they were standing to one another, they'd reached a turning point, and it was a bittersweet realisation to know that they'd finally come together when I was about to lose Xavier for good. Even if the Grim Reaper did wake up from his coma, the Council would end us without a doubt.

I could barely meet his eyes as I reached out to hand him the phoenix feather. He looked down at my hand without taking it. "Rory."

"Don't." My voice broke. "I know the Reaper Council will find out about my involvement no matter what, but there's no point in turning myself into their punching bag. Take the cure, wake up the others, and I'll come as soon as they call me."

"You don't have to," he insisted. "I saw almost everything. Just fill me in on the rest, and I'll give them the full story myself. You don't deserve to be subjected to another interrogation."

"Neither do you." I still hadn't told him precisely how I'd rescued him, and he at least deserved an explanation of how I'd learned of my unexpected ability to open the afterworld using my biblio-witch magic. "Also, there's one part that only I can explain."

And I told him. He listened in shocked silence as I recounted how I'd found my way to his side and transported us back to the library.

"How can that be possible?" he murmured. "A family of humans gaining access to the afterworld is supposed to be forbidden."

"That's the other thing I never had time to tell you," I said. "I found out my grandma briefly trained as a Reaper apprentice, long before I was born."

"Who told you that?"

"Well… Reid did," I admitted. "But it makes sense, given the other secrets Grandma kept. How else would our magic be able to affect the afterworld?"

What would his boss think about that? Nothing good, I assumed.

"We'll have to talk about it more later," he said. "I *will* come back, Rory. I promise I will."

———

IF NOT FOR my sheer exhaustion, I might have been more worried that the Reaper Council might descend upon the library in the middle of the night. As it was, I felt hollow, numb, and caught between relief at Xavier's recovery and fear that I'd already been too late for the others.

The library kept me busy for the rest of the evening, between the sheer chaos that Reid's imprisonment had left behind and Aunt Candace's lingering curiosity over Grandma's apparent escapades in the afterworld. She reluctantly obeyed Aunt Adelaide's rule to refrain from opening the afterworld in the library, though some of that might have been because the guardian spent the rest of the night lingering in the lobby, as if to keep an eye on us.

As for me, I escaped to my room for an early night and, to my own surprise, passed out cold into a dreamless sleep.

I woke to a chorus of loud carol singing from Sylvester, who'd perched at the top of the stairs to serenade everyone who walked past.

"Someone needs to get into the holiday spirit." He pursued me into the kitchen and settled on top of a cupboard. "It's positively maudlin in here."

"That'd be because the library had to play host to a Reaper apprentice who also happened to be a murderer." I sank down into a seat at the table and helped myself to some toast and coffee. "And, you know, some of us nearly got murdered ourselves."

"But you didn't," he said. "The Reapers are back to their usual grumpy selves, and we no longer have to entertain their presence here. Isn't that reason enough to celebrate?"

"You might have offered a hand in capturing Reid." I yawned. "Wouldn't the Forbidden Room be an ideal place to imprison a Reaper somewhere he couldn't get out?"

"You seemed to be managing just fine on your own."

"And did you know we could use our Biblio-Witch Inventories to access the afterworld?" I had a difficult time believing he hadn't, not with how close he'd been to the library's creation. "Because that seems like something you ought to have mentioned earlier."

"I am hardly to blame for your lack of imagination," he retorted, and I dropped the subject, not having the heart to argue.

Since it was Christmas Eve, the library was due to be closed for the next three days. Estelle suggested we watch some Christmas movies and that I invite Cass and Laney along too, and I was halfway through coming up with a half-hearted excuse when there came a knock on the door.

Xavier. I approached the door, my heart twisting into a painful knot. He'd told me he'd come back, even if it was to say goodbye.

And he wasn't alone. The Grim Reaper stood as tall and shadowy as ever, back to full strength, and I couldn't help feeling some measure of relief despite myself. Even if Xavier and I were doomed to be torn apart, he wouldn't have to take his supervisor's place for a while yet.

"What are you doing here?" I swallowed around the lump in my throat. "Do the Council want to speak to me?"

"No," said the Grim Reaper. "Due to no small effort on my part, I convinced them that the library was only a small part of the events of the previous few days and that the priority should be ensuring the prisoner was contained and that any potions he had in his possession were confiscated."

It took several moments for the impact of his words to sink in. "What do you want, then?"

"To tell you they've gone." Xavier reached out a hand and took mine, heedless of his boss's disapproving air. "They took Reid with them, and Janus went too. They're calling in all the Reapers to question individually."

My heart slammed against my ribs, and I didn't quite dare pull him any closer. "Including you? And... me?"

"No," he said. "My boss managed to get them to keep you out of it. They have no idea you were involved."

My mouth parted in disbelief. "The other Reapers agreed? Even Freya?"

"I asked her to, as a favour to you," said the Grim Reaper, sounding as if it pained him to admit. "For saving the Reapers and capturing the traitor."

"He means he's grateful," Xavier added. "Enough to bend the rules a little."

"Bend the rules." I didn't know whether to cry or laugh. "We've already done plenty of that by letting me get involved in the first place."

"Reid is the one who deserves punishment, not you," said Xavier. "I held off on waking all the others until after the Council took him away. That gave my boss the time to come up with our cover story."

To protect me... and to keep the others from revealing the truth. My eyes stung with tears. "I'm glad everyone's all right. Even Janus. He's not locked up anymore?"

"He is not," said the Grim Reaper. "As he was clearly innocent of any crime, I saw no problem in letting him walk free."

"Good." Now that my disbelief had begun to turn to hope, some of my lingering questions returned to the forefront of my mind. "Ah… did Xavier mention I opened the afterworld using my biblio-witch magic?"

A dangerous stillness came over him. "That should not be possible."

"But it is." I scrambled to phrase my question in the right way, not wanting to drive him into a fury and burn the temporary truce between us. "Reid told me that you offered to take on my grandmother as an apprentice, years ago. Maybe that's why."

His tone turned icy cold. "Now is not the time for this conversation."

I should have seen that one coming. "Not now, but my family and I want to know the truth. We wouldn't have been able to capture Reid and save your lives without access to that magic, so it's only fair."

"You will get your answers," he said, "at a time when this matter is long behind us."

"I'll hold you to that." I would, and who knew, maybe he'd

move up the timeline the next time Aunt Candace inevitably got curious enough to open the afterworld using our family's magic.

In the meantime, though, I'd let him be. He'd stuck his neck out for me in a major way, done the impossible, and ensured I got to spend the holidays with Xavier without the Council tearing us apart.

I'd never take that for granted again.

THE OTHER REAPERS departed on the last day of the year. Xavier and I went to see them off on our way to the celebration at the pier, when most of the town's population would gather to see in the new year.

"I owe your family for saving us all from that little weasel, Reid," Alise said. "I never liked him. I should have known he was up to no good."

"He took us all by surprise," I said. "Even his master."

"Janus is used to losing apprentices by now," Alise said wryly. "If nothing else, the curse will probably stop now that Reid's in the Council's prison, where he belongs."

Lara muttered something uncomplimentary under her breath. She'd accompanied her fellow apprentices to the library though she kept her distance from Alise while they waited for their supervisors to join them. She'd been oddly subdued since waking from her coma, and Alise had told me in confidence that even Freya hadn't had any idea that Reid was the true mastermind until he'd nearly killed all of them.

"I think the Council gave everyone a good scare," Alise had added, "including her. They'll have dragged up her history with the vampires, too, and given Gwyn a stern talking-to about that beast of his."

Since Hunt had actually been responsible for helping

Janus escape his prison and fetch help, Gwyn had been allowed to keep his pet—with conditions. When I spied the other Reapers approaching our group, the large wolfhound was wearing an equally large collar and harness as Gwyn led him along.

"Ready?" Val waved to her apprentice. "Nice meeting you, Rory. You made this a very interesting trip."

"I hope the good outweighed the bad." I smiled back at her and waved goodbye to Alise as they both vanished in a dramatic swirl of shadows.

The others did not offer a goodbye. Gwyn and Janus departed one by one, then Freya beckoned her apprentice to follow her into the darkness. That left the Grim Reaper, who gave his apprentice one of his long, unreadable looks before vanishing too.

"Guess he's not going to stay and watch the fireworks." I slid my hand into Xavier's, and he and I walked to the pier to join the others.

On the surface, the scene was the same as the previous year, crowds of people wrapped up in warm layers, gathering at the seafront, watching the night sky—a familiar picture with some crucial differences. For one, Xavier and I weren't apart but closer than ever. Cass didn't stand alone this time but side by side with Laney. *In fact... are they holding hands?*

Cass caught me watching and turned her head. "Good, you're here. Thought you were going to miss the first shooting star."

"That's right." I found a free spot for Xavier and me to stand in. "Did you know that the witches say you should make a wish on the first star that appears at the new year?"

He squeezed my hand. "I heard about the tradition, but I can't say I've ever done it before."

"There's a first time for everything." I lifted my gaze to the sky. "Last year... I wished for you."

He lowered his lips to mine and murmured, "I'm glad it came true."

"Me too."

As for next year, it might be impossible to look any further ahead than that, but I hadn't given up on us having a real future together. If I'd learned anything in the past week, it was that anything was possible, even for a Reaper and a human.

As I watched the first star begin to fall, I held Xavier's hand, knowing we'd both made the exact same wish, the same wish we'd make every year until it came true.

ABOUT THE AUTHOR

Elle Adams lives in the middle of England, where she spends most of her time reading an ever-growing mountain of books, planning her next adventure, or writing. Elle's books are humorous mysteries with a paranormal twist, packed with magical mayhem.

She also writes urban and contemporary fantasy novels as Emma L. Adams.

Find Elle on Facebook at https://www.facebook.com/pg/ElleAdamsAuthor/